An Inconvenient Monday

A DS Henry Stafford Mystery

Ginette Guy Mayer

Also by Ginette Guy Mayer

An Elizabeth Grant Mystery Series

A Peculiar Case

The Gale

The Literary Thread

A DS Henry Stafford Mystery Series

An Inconvenient Monday

Destiny Dictates (release date early 2024)

Other

Unforgotten Mary Mack Cornwall's First Lady

Livres en français

Une enquête d'Élizabeth Grant

Un cas particulier

La tourmente

Le fil littéraire

Acknowledgement

A big thanks to Paul R. King for keeping a keen eye on the commas and the dots. And, for his encouragement with all my writing projects. To all the friends who comment and review, thank you for your patience.

Thank you to all the characters in this book who think nothing of waking me up at 4 am because they have something clever to say.

Note to the reader

This novel is set in the mid-1980s in Winchester and Chesterville and the Counties of Stormont, Dundas and Glengarry. It's important to note that the novel is a work of fiction, and any resemblance to actual police operations or organizational structures of that era has been intentionally altered to accommodate the imaginative narrative.

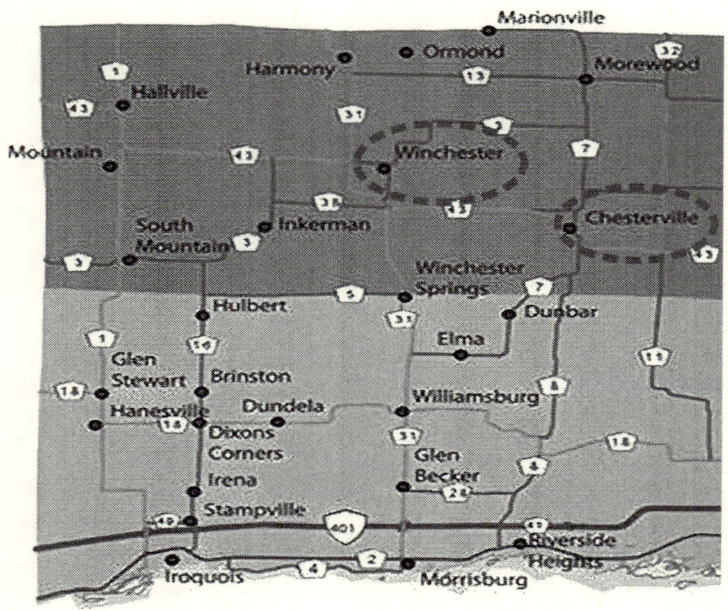
Marionville
Ormond
Harmony
Morewood
Hallville
Mountain
Winchester
Chesterville
South Mountain
Inkerman
Winchester Springs
Hulbert
Dunbar
Elma
Glen Stewart
Brinston
Williamsburg
Hanesville
Dundela
Dixons Corners
Glen Becker
Irena
Stampville
401
Riverside Heights
Iroquois
Morrisburg

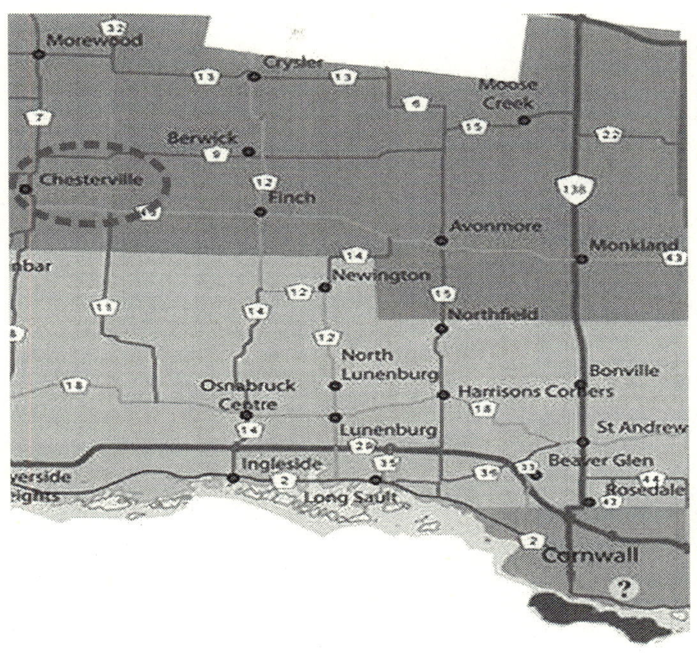
Morewood
Crysler
Moose Creek
Berwick
Chesterville
Finch
Avonmore
Monkland
Newington
Northfield
North Lunenburg
Bonville
Osnabruck Centre
Harrisons Corners
Lunenburg
St Andrew
Ingleside
Beaver Glen
Rosedale
Long Sault
Cornwall
?

First Edition 2023

www.ginetteguymayer.com
ginetteguymayer@gmail.com

Cover design by Ginette Guy Mayer
Using Postermywall.com & Canva
Photo from Pexels.com Amina Filkins

ISBN 978-1-7380450-7-5 (Paperback)
ISBN 978-1-7380450-8-2 (eBook)
ISBN 978-1-7380450-9-9 (Large Print Paperback)

Chapter 1

When the Happiness Train left the station, little Henry James Stafford quickly realized that he didn't have a first-class ticket. His boarding pass must have been rebated from a fire sale because it took him past the "satisfied" section into the "barely content" section. And that's where he sat for most of his life.

Of course, he had moved up to "content" a few times, like when he got married, but was quickly brought back down to his designated spot just before the caboose. Once, he even peeked into the window of "happiness" but that was brief, he didn't have enough joy to enter, let alone take a seat.

But he wasn't unhappy, that would have required a deeper analysis of his life and he just couldn't be bothered to expend the energy. He did most things because they were in front of him, within reach and uncomplicated.

He was the middle child of a large family, lost in the shuffle of the others, not doing enough either bad or good to be noticeable. He didn't make waves, rather he bobbed along down the river until a friend from high school told him he was going to be a policeman. Henry Stafford followed him to the provincial police recruiting office. Being of average height, build and ability, he got in as a recruit. He graduated without honours but finished tenth in a class of twenty.

The graduating class went out to celebrate at Logan's Hotel and his friend Harvey introduced him to his girlfriend's sister, Paula. Henry didn't have to do much aside from smiling, as Paula already had plans for a man in uniform with a steady income. Henry was drawn to the edge of the "happiness" window when Paula's charms showed him what nature and a few beers could do. But to get, Henry had to give, and marriage was the only thing Paula understood. So, wedded bliss being the logical next step, Henry fell in line. The initial stages of marriage brought him directly to the "content" car. A few years later, after the nagging and belittling, he went down to "barely content." Only his ability to adapt and find solace in routine spared him from a stint in the "depressed" section.

They had no children, and that kept Henry in the last car of the Happiness Train for many years. Still, he went on, day to day, with perfect attendance at work, doing what was expected. Doing well enough in fact, that when openings occurred, he wrote a few exams and gained a promotion. He was now a Detective Sergeant, taking roots at the Winchester station. He became, quite without effort or intention, a leader of men. In a streak of luck, he assembled a team that liked to manage themselves, requiring only the annual performance evaluation in the way of administration.

One rainy day in November, Paula packed a suitcase and left with Edgar the next-door neighbour. Henry received a postcard from Saskatchewan, they had opened a diner and she asked Henry to send her cooking books. That evening, when he packed the books, so new the spine cracked when you opened them, he laughed for a solid half hour. There was an oxymoron here somewhere, he thought, sipping his beer. Paula, and cooking and a diner business, was the funniest thing he ever imagined. Her cooking had been so bad that the guys at the station used to pool their resources and give him pieces of their lunches. That's how sorry they felt for him!

Edgar's wife also received a note, hers was a letter from the bank saying their joint account was overdrawn. Unable to sell the house independently, she decided to rent it and go live with her ageing mother. As a final farewell, she took Henry to bed, not because she liked him, but rather as something owed her, revenge. Henry, only wanting to be accommodating, went along with it. He didn't have the heart to tell her that as far as revenge went, nobody cared. The next morning, she left and never looked back.

With their respective spouses gone, Edgar's wife had lost her meal ticket, and Henry had lost a bad cook. He took it in stride. As a couple they never had a love life to speak of, rather some occasional shared intermissions, of no consequence. As fair-minded as he was, Henry would never have blamed her for that. With no bond between them, it was like putting two ice cubes side-by-each and expecting one to melt the other.

Now in his early forties, he clung to "content" only because of his hobbies. Henry Stafford spent his off-duty time on two things, building a boat in his garage and collecting old photographs. The boat building was a recent undertaking. On a cold December afternoon, out on a job in Ottawa, he'd seen the W. Farmer's *How to Build 20 Boats*, in a used bookstore window. He went in, picked it up and while he noticed R.M. Bealer's *Problems in Boat Making*, he left that one on the shelf, why jinx it?

The detached garage, at the end of his driveway, was not heated so he started the boat building in his basement, with obvious limitations. That winter he built a model and ordered additional blueprints. The *Badger,* a fifteen-foot modified dory would be built over the summer, so he planned. One could question an interest in boat building from someone who had never been on a boat and who did not live near water. If this was not enough, his other passion was a complete head-scratcher for the few who knew about it. Henry collected old photographs, more precisely vintage portraits of people he didn't know.

The pursuit of the unknown faces had started soon after he was married. The need to get out of the stifling home, paired with a work assignment, led him to flea markets and pawn shops. Stolen items were often passed on to street dealers, armed with a list of goods he snooped around. Rows of stalls sold everything from hubcaps to houseware, most of it bought in turns by hoarders. One table though caught his attention, more vintage jewellery and antiques, and in the corner was a small, framed portrait of a beautiful young lady. Faded black and white, a shy smile gazed at him from the 1890s. He bought it. That summer Constable Stafford recovered more stolen items than any other police officer in the department while spending a small fortune on what he considered art.

Like an addict looking for a fix, he grew his network of suppliers, all of whom knew him and kept the best pieces for him. He catalogued the portraits, adding any little bits of information he could find, with the idea that for some he would find a relative and return them. If framed he would take them apart and see if anything was inscribed on the back of the photo, a name, a photographer, a place. When time allowed, he would run the names he'd found through the police database, missing persons and cold cases, just to be thorough.

Chapter 2

At the beginning of March, in the early days of warmer weather, Henry changed places on the Happiness Train. He still stayed in the "content" section but moved from an aisle seat to a window seat. That change was brought about by spending a bit of money. While Henry knew that he could not advance to the full "happiness" section strictly via material things, an occasional bump-up was allowed.

After a sad December and a re-grouping in January and February, when March rolled along things were looking up. Henry had replaced Paula with a new Weber gas BBQ grill, complete with a side burner, and a weekly visit from the Molly Maid service. Overall, a massive improvement in the quality of his meals, so much so that now, his colleagues were begging for bits of his lunches!

He grilled everything, rain or shine. He placed trimmings and vegetables in little aluminium foil packets and practically eliminated dirty dishes, pots and pans. He even added a griddle plate so he could do bacon and eggs. He credited his move to the window seat to the fact that he now had the full run of the house. He put his feet on the coffee table and left the toilet seat up. In a show of bravado, he used some of Paula's Tupperware containers and lids to mix his paints and the epoxy for his boat.

He also Paula-proofed the house by getting two cats from the Ontario SPCA. Paula was deadly allergic to cats, so this ownership ensured she would never return to the house. Without the cats, he knew that should she show up, suitcase in hand, he would have let her in. Not because he wanted her back but because it would have been easy to do. Now fully attached to Oscar and KC, the bonded pair he had adopted, the choice between a perfidious wife and the furry companions was obvious.

The one thing he could not wrap his head around was that he was less lonely on his own than when he had been with Paula. He didn't drink much but on weekends he would pick up a six-pack of beer, grill, move his tools and boat-making supplies up to the garage and work on cataloguing his vintage portraits. He even imagined asking the guys from the station to come up for a barbecue this summer. On the occasional Sunday, he did the run of the antique shops he frequented on the lookout for more portraits. *Treasures to Share* in Chesterville, owned by Mary Blake, a divorcee, always had good finds. Mary had often offered to discount his purchases in exchange for certain personal services. Now that he was single, he reconsidered the offer. He never expected a large discount but it seemed to him a win-win situation. Given the proper prompts, it turned out his skills in that department were quite marketable, earning him full rebates on a few occasions.

The house next door, a mirror image of his, was now rented. With the dividing fence in the backyard and the garage at the opposite end, he never saw the tenants. They either worked nights or evenings. Now with the warmer weather, he had glimpsed at a child on a tricycle riding the length of the street. There might also have been a teenage boy around.

He worked on his boat again, opening the garage door to let the sun warm the interior and remove the dampness. The prep work seemed exhaustive and the progress was slow. He could tell when the little girl next door was out because the tricycle bell rang constantly as she went up and down the street. She looked to be five or six years old, it was hard to tell, she was small at any rate. She had brown shoulder-length hair, curly but mostly tangled in a mix of curls and knots. When he opened the garage door, he noticed that the bell ringing had stopped and that the bike was stationary at the end of his driveway with the kid looking in his direction. She didn't say hi, or even directly look at his face but she stared at the garage. He went on his business and she stayed there until a voice yelled out "Ellie" and she zoomed on, the bell ringing.

Work was going extremely well because there was nothing much to do, no calls, no emergencies. Murders and kidnappings were not a routine business in these parts, but they did have the occasional armed robbery, break-ins and some minor crimes to investigate. The uniformed constables dealt with traffic accidents and those could be heavy in bad weather. Within the East Region, the Winchester station covered a wide rural area and the towns of Chesterville and Winchester. Henry loved this posting.

Detective Sergeant Stafford had no qualms about a slow work week, month or year. He had nothing to prove, well honestly, he did, but he wasn't looking for a promotion. The respect he'd earned from his colleagues came from not getting anyone else in trouble, and not telling tales. He wouldn't turn a blind eye if one of his teammates was crooked or abusive but otherwise, it was live and let live. He worked with Detective Constable Patrick Jones, and this week they were hosting Detective Constable Randy Travers from the Long Sault station for training. Travers normally oversaw the crime scenes, taking photos and fingerprints.

Mid-afternoon on Friday, the boss came out to let them know that some people from IT would come in and set up a computer. The detachment would get one unit to start, progressing to a complete information management system to assist with investigations. For some, hell had just frozen over. They would eventually put computers in the patrol cars! Training would be scheduled for everyone.

"Any questions?" asked Staff Sergeant Glenn.

Travers raised his hand and said, "What's an IT?" The guys laughed and Staff Sergeant Glenn booked Travers on the first training session available.

By the end of the day, Henry had a small monitor on his desk and keyboard. This was going to shake his routine and he didn't like it.

"For the love of God," he whined. "I'll go blind looking at that small screen all day. Come back here with my typewriter! Thank God, it's Friday!"

Over the next weeks, they were busy at work with computer training and Henry adapted to the changes relatively well. He caught on and liked the logic of it all. He could see how helpful the use of computers would be, if they worked well, of course. This was not always the case and the IT people, information technology he learned, were on call around the clock. It was one of those transitions, but for Henry, his fatalistic approach to life turned out to be an asset.

Henry also found the trick around IT. Since any call for support would start with "Did you turn it on and off?" he had his own diagnostic process before he placed the call. This earned him the respect of that department. They were more likely to return his calls promptly!

Of course, it was not in Henry's nature to put himself forward. He didn't get in anybody's way but if someone asked, he helped as best he could. There was a boost in the way the guys appreciated him. Over the last months, Jones and Travers had also seen a bit of a change in Henry.

"You noticed Stafford seems more relaxed these days?" whispered Travers. His metal desk faced Jones while Henry was set up on his own further down.

"Yep, ever since the wife left him!" Jones laughed.

"Thank God for small mercies," said Travers aloud. "I only met her once and that was enough for me. Christ, remember that time we went for a beer and she joined us?"

"Yes, that was embarrassing," confided Jones. "The whole evening, she told stories that made

Henry look bad and called him numb nuts and an idiot. I felt sorry for the guy."

"No wonder he's in a better mood, bye bye Paula!" said Travers.

Asking no more of his Monday morning than a powdered doughnut and a strong coffee, Henry jumped when the phone rang. It was the administrative clerk at the front. The local hospital had a run-in with a patient last night, allegedly wounded by a bullet. It was a duty to notify the police anytime something like that happened. It was he and Jones in the office, so he called him over.

"Jones," said Stafford. "Want to come with me to the Winchester Hospital? We have a gunshot injury."

"Now?" questioned Jones. "I've just started the crosswords!"

Patrick Jones had just over ten years in, he was in his thirties, tall, slim as a pole with reddish hair. Sideways he looked like a Redbird matchstick. In contrast, DS Stafford was about five feet nine inches, a bit on the heavy side, from years of snacking from the station vending machines. Behind their backs, the guys called them Abbott and Costello.

"Come on, let's go," said Stafford. "If you wait for tomorrow's paper, you'll get the answers to today's puzzle anyway."

They could've crossed the street and walked over to the hospital, but two policemen arriving on foot didn't look very official. They drove the two-minutes it took, considering the oncoming traffic and parked in the no-parking zone beside the entrance. Stafford and Jones went directly to the emergency room. The nurse at the desk, a late thirties, lightly chunky brunette looked up at them with a raised eyebrow. She was wearing a Mickey Mouse print scrub top, with Mickey's yellow shoes dancing on the grey background.

"I'm Detective Sergeant Henry Stafford, and this is Detective Constable Jones." Each showed their badge.

She gave him the once over and assumed he was single or that his wife didn't like him much if he had one. No self-respecting woman would let her man walk out of the house dressed like that. DS Stafford made loose-fitting an art form, and he took it to the next level. He was a brown smudge, with pants too high at the waist, a wrinkled shirt in white, and an open jacket with a green tie. Give him a pork pie hat and he'd be Yogi Bear! She'd hate to give in to stereotypes but was that a light dusting from a powdered doughnut on his tie wondered the nurse.

"You reported a gunshot wound?" asked Stafford. Jones opened a small notebook and clicked his ballpoint.

"Yes, I'm the one that phoned it in," said the nurse. "Of course, he's long gone now, he ran away with gauze and tape."

"May I have your name and contact information for our files, please?" asked Jones.

"Sure, I'm Lisa Stuart, at 449 Clarence Street, here in Winchester."

Henry didn't say anything but recognized the address as being the house next to his. She was the new tenant.

"Mrs Stuart, could you tell me more about the patient, time of arrival, condition, everything you noticed," said Stafford.

"It's Miss…" she started. "He arrived last evening, towards the end of my shift, around 11:30. He was a walk-in, no ambulance. He was bleeding heavily and we took him directly to a stretcher in emergency."

"Did you get a name, a description?" asked Stafford.

"Just a first name, Alex," said Nurse Stuart. "He looked about 19 or 20, about your height, slim, black hair. He was wearing jeans, a jean jacket, you know the one with a fleece lining. And of course, a blood-soaked t-shirt. The priority was to deal with the injury, I never got a chance to do the processing, he left before we were done."

"How badly hurt was he?" asked Jones, clicking his pen repeatedly.

"The bullet's trajectory resulted in a superficial injury," said Nurse Stuart. "It was on his left side, with no tissue or organ damage. The bullet went right through. I cleaned the wound, dressed it and gave him a painkiller. I left his bedside to get some antibiotics when I returned, he had left and taken some supplies with him."

"You don't have a bullet then? Do you think he will need more care later, could he need to see a doctor?" asked Stafford.

"Unless it gets infected, he should be fine," she replied. "He would have to be careful not to tear the stitches and have more bleeding."

"Thank you for this information," said Stafford. "We will see if anyone else reported anything suspicious in the area. So, you're on shift today and worked last evening?"

"Yes, I normally do evenings or nights, but they were short today and called me in," replied Nurse Stuart.

Stafford and Jones walked to their police car, drove across the street and parked at the station. "What do you think about this one?" asked Stafford.

"I'm thinking that 'wound' is five down in today's crossword," said Jones.

"Idiot," said Stafford. He went to the coffee maker to grab his fourth cup of the morning. "Do you want to draft the report? I'll check last night's log to see if there were any incidents written up."

Henry picked up the log from Sunday and threw it on his desk. Facing this type of workload, he decided to go for lunch first. He wasn't much good on an empty stomach. When he came back, he ploughed through and noticed there had been a call from someone claiming to have heard a gunshot on Main Street around eleven that evening. Officers were dispatched but nothing suspicious was found and no one was on the scene. They didn't have a gang problem in town, but things were changing. Also noted was a stolen 1983 Black Chevrolet Caprice called in by William Campbell Sunday evening.

The rest of the week was spent under the sound of computers being turned on and off and faint cursing from his fellow officers. The IT crew was still packed in the computer room. An empty office had been re-purposed with refrigerator-size boxes lining the wall. All had little lights flashing. The room was permanently air-conditioned. Two of the boxes had windows showing reel-to-reel tapes for data storage, the IT crew had explained to Henry.

"Stafford," yelled Travers. "There's a message for you."

"Sure, give it to me, at 4:30, on a Friday, won't you," said an exasperated Henry. "I'd bet you've been sitting on it for the last half hour, haven't you?"

"No, honest, you know me better than that," said Travers, with the most offended look on his face. "It's an insurance adjuster, a guy on Main put in a claim on his insurance for damage to his car."

"And…do I look like I do bodywork and paint?" asked Henry.

"No, it was a bullet that damaged the car and the bullet is still in there," explained Travers. "Here's the name, phone and address. The insurance guy said he'd be there until five."

"I'm on my way, and I'm not coming back, I'll write it up on Monday," said Henry.

Henry made his way to Main Street, at the number on the piece of paper, it was the funeral parlour. A car was parked in the back, with two men looking around at it, taking photos and notes.

"Hi, I'm Detective Sergeant Stafford, you phoned about a bullet."

"Yes, I'm Mark Pryce, from Allstate Insurance. The car belongs to William Campbell, he had reported it stolen on Sunday night.

"Yes, I saw the police report," said Stafford.

"The owner of the funeral parlour called the police station to report a car that had been sitting here all week. The constable called Mr Campbell to let him know his car was here," said Pryce. He was going to take it home when he noticed the damage. He wasn't sure about moving the car, so he called us with a claim. He thought vandalism, but when I began to do the appraisal, it was clear it was a bullet and it's still in the trunk."

"Thanks, it's good of you to have called us and not taken it out," said Stafford. "I have an evidence bag; I'll get gloves and take it away to be matched. This is helpful, we've had another incident on Sunday, perhaps the two are related."

Henry took the bullet; it looked like a 9mm. Despite what he had said to Travers, he did go back to the station and turned it in for processing. He would draft the report on Monday, but he couldn't see walking around all weekend with a bullet in his pocket. It wasn't proper procedure.

Chapter 3

Bright and early every Saturday, the weekend edition of the Ottawa Citizen was thrown at Henry's door. He had a subscription for that day only and flipped through the various sections over morning coffee. He always put aside the tv listings insert. On Monday he would give the insert to Jones, his colleague, so that he could copy his selected line-up. Jones was too cheap to buy the newspaper.

It rained all of Saturday and the forecast was no better for Sunday. Henry decided to drop by the antique shops and see if anything new had come in. Everything he had now was a dead-end, he hadn't identified anyone for months now. He planned to visit *Treasures To Share* and the friendly Mary in Chesterville. Who knew, she might be in a mood for negotiations, so he dabbed on a few extra drops of aftershave. He opted for khaki pants with a plaid flannel shirt and rolled up his sleeves. Mary's store was his third visit for the day, the others had not yielded anything of interest. He hoped this last stop would prove better and not a total waste of his Sunday.

Chesterville was only about ten minutes southeast of Winchester. Mary Blake's shop was on

King Street, at the junction between Main, Water and King Streets, with a view of the South Nation River that ran through town. The shop was beside a restaurant. The neighbourhood was a favourite with Sunday strollers and tourists. Mary smiled when she saw him come in. The antique store was bursting at the seams. It was the sort of place you couldn't fully take in from the door. You had to weave through the open spaces between glass cabinets, shelves and hutches. If you noticed the larger pieces, you soon realized that each held a treasure trove of smaller items.

Mary was busy with a young couple looking at a vintage oil lamp and quickly closed the deal. Henry looked around the shop and glanced at Mary. She was in her late forties, and always went for the bohemian look, long earrings, blond hair down her back, although Henry knew she was not a natural blonde. She completed the look with long flowing skirts and colourful shirts, necklaces and chains. She had a good figure, but it wasn't immediately obvious because her clothes were always loose-fitting. Mary looked like she had just come back from Woodstock.

"Well, hello Henry, it's been a while," said Mary as she locked the door and turned the sign to the 'Sorry we're closed' side.

"I've been busy. It's nice to see you," said Henry. "Did anything interesting come into the shop?

"I was going to call you, I have something intriguing for you," said Mary. "It's in the back," leading and holding open the curtain to the private area and office. The rear of the shop was a standard office layout, with a desk, typewriter and filing cabinets. The only thing that set it apart was the presence of a large sofa on the left hand along the wall. It was comfortable and served many purposes as Henry knew.

Mary showed him a full box of photos, all assorted sizes, ranging from the late 1890s to the 1950s.

"Oh, that is interesting," said Henry.

More intriguing to him was the collection of military photos, from both World Wars. Some postcards and cabinet cards had the name of the photographer and addresses. Henry was hooked, he wanted the box. There were hours of work in there, and he was excited about the possibilities.

"I could sell them separately," said Mary, "but there isn't a lot of profit in photos, and there are too many that don't seem that vintage. I should sell them as a lot."

"How did you acquire them?" he asked.

"Henry, you know my stuff is always legit," replied Mary. "A guy from Cornwall, I know you're going to say it's a bit far to come and sell here. But he said he had family nearby. He had an I.D. and said the box had been left behind in a moving van. Unclaimed for a long time, and he needed to clear space. I thought of you straight away." She gave him one of her sexy smiles.

As customers go, Mary liked Henry, he was fair and never tried to get the upper hand in a deal. He was sweet so she took him on as a client with benefits. Timid at first, he now far exceeded her initial expectations.

"This is great," said Henry. "I would try to hide my enthusiasm but you know me better than that, how much?"

"I can already feel your interest," said Mary as she leaned in closer to him. "I believe we can come to an arrangement, which will work for both of us."

And they did…Henry walked out of *Treasures to Share*, with a banker's box full of photos. He had worked hard to barter a good deal. Over the time he had known Mary, Henry had considered calling her for a meal or a proper date. But he didn't want to mix business with pleasure, he rationalized. Should something go wrong with the relationship, he risked losing a good supplier. Better leave things as they were, he expected she had other "good" customers in her books.

He had one more stop to make, another purchase, and then home. He parked his old Chevrolet Biscayne in the driveway and headed for the basement with his parcels.

Henry enjoyed his work well enough but lived for his time off and away from the station. He now had plenty to keep him occupied, his new box of photos, pieces of wood yet to be assembled as a boat and a new computer for his home office. The cats looked at him adoringly, no matter what he wore. He started his weekend with sixties music rocking out of his boombox.

Henry went up to the kitchen to get a beer and glanced out his patio door to the backyard. He noticed a small fading red dot, and within seconds it glowed again. He turned on the outside light and a lanky teenager dropped the cigarette and moved back out of the light. Henry opened the door and yelled, "Hey, what are you doing there?" There was no answer so Henry walked out on the deck.

"You the kid next door, sneaking in my yard to hide a smoke?" asked Henry. Still no answer but the boy had not moved. He looked to be about thirteen or fourteen years old. Henry recognized him as the kid who hung around with the little brown-haired girl next door. Her brother he figured.

"You should probably save your money for something better than cigarettes," Henry snarled.

"Like what?" said the kid.

"Beer and women," replied Henry. The kid moved forward into the light and looked up at Henry, totally confused about this piece of advice. "What?" the kid said.

"Just kidding, at least try and spend your money on something that won't kill you," said Henry. "Cigarettes are bad for you, come to think of it, so is beer and women are risky as well."

The kid took a few steps, shaking his head, "You're weird, man," he said.

"What's your name? Are you the kid next door?" asked Henry.

"Yeah, but I'm not a kid," he protested. "I'm Jeremy."

"Do you know anything about computers, Sir?" smiled Henry.

"Yeah, we have them at school," said Jeremy, evaluating his chances of not getting into trouble and not having this neighbour report him to his mother.

"Can you help me with something? Come in," signalled Henry as he walked back into the house.

Jeremy followed hesitantly. "You're the policeman, right?"

"Yes, do you want a drink?" asked Henry stopping by the refrigerator.

"Sure. I'll have a beer," smiled Jeremy.

"I'll overlook the smoking, but I'm not your bartender. Pepsi?" He handed him a can and took one for himself.

"My stuff is downstairs," and Henry led the way to the stairs leading to the basement.

"I got a Commodore 64, got it out of the box, connected everything, the little tv screen is on and all I have is this blue screen with a small square flashing," explained Henry. "Oh, I'm Henry by the way."

Jeremy looked at the set-up on the small desk and took the wires out of some coloured holes to place them in other coloured holes. He turned everything back on.

"You need to get yourself a joystick," commented Jeremy.

"No dirty talk in my house," said Henry.

"No, you don't have a clue, do you?" sighed Jeremy.

"See the flashing square is on again, on the tv screen, it says "Commodore 64 Basic V2 64K RAM system 38911 Basic Bytes Free Ready"…Ready for what?" asked Henry.

"Ok, so first, the screen is not a little tv, it's a monitor, then you have the keyboard and the floppy disk drive, those are the hardware," said Jeremy.

Henry noticed the kid was using the same tone of voice he used when explaining something to his five-year-old sister.

"We just got computers at work, but there's more stuff on the screen, I don't get this," said Henry. "The training was all about what to do after you turned it on, not how it's built."

"That's because at work you have software," Jeremy glanced up and realized he might just as well have been talking about calculus, Henry had no light in his eyes. "When you buy a thing like this, it's bare, empty, no programming."

"For the hardware to do things, you need something inside, software, like a heart and brain…get it?" asked Jeremy. "Oh, my god…" he continued. "This box here holds the floppy disk, on the floppy disk is where the software is, it tells the computer…what to do."

"So, what is the joystick thingy, you were talking about?" asked Henry.

"It would allow you to play games, you have a slot for cartridges here in the back. What did you plan to do with this anyway, what is it for?" asked Jeremy, by now he was not expecting miracles.

"I have a collection of old photos," said Henry. "And I thought I could use this to catalogue them. It's a little like how we use the computer at work, to get information out of it."

"Ok, I see," said Jeremy. "But it's getting late and I have to get home, my mother is working night and I have to stay with my sister."

"Can you come back another day and help me out? I'm not stupid you know, I'm sure I can make sense of it."

"Sure, it's yours now, so you might as well learn," said Jeremy encouragingly. "I can come back another evening."

"Thanks, much appreciated. I can do snacks next time."

"Chips and beer," said Jeremy.

"Get out of here," laughed Henry as he pulled the plug on the computer and the flashing square faded to black.

Sunny Sunday was reserved for the boat, or some sort of work with wood and tools. The jury was still out on whether these efforts would ever float. Henry opened the garage door and heard the bell of the tricycle once again. By now it was background noise, and he turned on his portable radio to the local station. The little girl passed by twenty or more times before turning into his driveway, up to his car bumper and down again. Henry noticed that one of her back wheels was dangerously wobbly.

"Hey kid," he yelled. But she continued up and down.

"Your bike is broken," yelled Henry. This had an effect and she came up sitting behind his car, her front wheel the only thing in view. He walked over and said, "Can I look at your bike, one of your wheels is falling off."

"No, it's not," she said. "Yes, it is," said Henry. Then she noticed the cat, Oscar lounging on the first step to his deck. She got off the bike and asked, "Can I pet the kitty?"

"Sure," said Henry, "just be gentle." He took the bike and looked at the wheel. He brought pliers, a wrench and a couple of washers to stabilize it.

"Ellie, Ellie," came a shout, from her mother. "Where are you?"

"I'm here Mommy," yelled the kid, scaring the cat, who took shelter in the garage.

The mother came over, and Henry did recognize her as the nurse from last Monday's call at the Winchester Hospital. She was wearing jeans and a sweatshirt, with a Minnie Mouse print on the front. A definite pattern was emerging, thought Henry.

"Look Mommy, the old man has a kitty," said the girl.

The mother looked at Henry with an apologetic smile and said, "I'm so sorry, for her anyone over the age of 10 is old!"

"I know I didn't shave…but," said Henry. Now, she was looking at him more closely.

"Hi, I recognize you," said Nurse Stuart. "You're the policeman from the bullet call!"

"Yes, Henry Stafford. And you're Lisa Stuart if memory serves. Your daughter's bike had a wheel coming loose, so I fixed it."

"Thank you very much, I'm no good at these things," she said.

"Come on Ellie, time to go in for lunch," said Lisa.

"I hope you won't mind but your son is helping me with my new computer," said Henry. "Just so it's ok with you."

"Sure, if he can help, it'll keep him out of trouble," said Lisa. "He's a good kid, but when I saw that nineteen-year-old with the bullet through him, I couldn't help but worry about him. Getting in with the wrong crowd and such."

"Well, I don't know if I'm the right crowd, but he's just next door and home early," laughed Henry. Ellie jumped back on her bike and rang the bell all the way home, her mother beside her. Henry looked at them walk away and nothing, absolutely nothing, came to his mind. Where another might have seen opportunity in a pleasant single neighbour, Henry, fateful to who he was, didn't risk opportunities.

Chapter 4

Henry was starting to hate Mondays, all those early morning calls lately, not even a minute to enjoy his coffee. And here he was again, 10 am and someone was yelling his name across the office. A call for him just came in.

"DS Stafford here, what can I do for you?" answered Henry.

"Hi Henry, it's Mary, from the antique shop. I've had a theft."

"Ok, are you alright?" asked Henry.

"Yes, I'm fine, thank you for asking," replied Mary. "The thing is I'm not sure exactly when it happened. You know the shop, there's stuff everywhere and I don't do regular inventories."

"Are there any signs of a break-in, broken window, forced entry?" asked Henry. "Is anything much missing?"

"No, the problem is that I have a small handgun, it's in a locked metal box, but now it's gone," said Mary.

"I'll be right over and we can look at it," said Henry. "Was it registered?" He didn't say the word "gun" because he didn't want to draw attention in case it wasn't legally owned.

"I'm afraid not Henry. That's why I thought it better to call you first," confided Mary.

Mary knew she could trust Henry. She liked him from the start. Initially, he had resisted her advances, almost running out of the shop after every purchase. Then one day last fall, she noticed he wasn't wearing his wedding ring anymore and stayed a bit longer. It was like he had permitted himself to enjoy their friendship. Mary always planned to have the items he was interested in stored in the office. It was clear to her that as a husband and lover, he had been underutilized. He was gentle and eager to please. A lot of the men she knew were more forward. Now the tables were turned on her and she relished it. It always ended up that the photos he liked needed a finer inspection, her getting closer, reaching in. But Henry was no fool, and he caught on right away. But still, they enjoyed the game, even when the ending was a foregone conclusion.

Henry stuffed gloves and a few evidence bags into his jacket pockets and left for Chesterville. It took about half an hour for Henry to reach the antique shop by the time he picked up a coffee to go and told Jones where he was going. The street was quiet, being early on a Monday. He entered the shop but Mary did not come forward so he assumed she was in the back. There was a bell at the door that announced visitors, so he expected her to come to the front quickly. The layout of the store was simple, with merchandise filling every inch from the store entrance to the back. At the opposite end was the cash register sitting atop a glass display case, which contained the more expensive pieces. Just behind was a doorway leading to the back office, it was separated by a curtain. He called out her name but there was no reply. He made his way towards the back. And there she was, on the ground, in front of the display case. Her body was still and her head rested in a pool of blood. He bent down and touched her, looking for a sign of life, but nothing.

"Oh, God, this is going to be paperwork," he murmured. He shook himself, as inconvenient as this was for him, it was much worse for Mary Blake. He put on gloves and called Jones. He asked for the full team, coroner and crime scene investigation. He looked at Mary and felt sick. He went outside to wait for the guys and took a deep breath.

When Jones arrived, Henry filled him in on the original call. The uniform constable secured the scene and taped off the area. Henry stood at the door with Travers and Jones behind him. They couldn't all go trampling in there, the shop was small and Travers would dust for prints and take photos.

Travers, showing off keen observation skills said, "Obviously it's theft!"

"Is that so?" said Henry. "Are you thinking she got burglarized, called me to report it, half an hour ago and got burglarized again, while she waited for me?"

"Well, when you put it like that. Maybe not," conceded Travers.

"I come to this shop, I know her," said Henry. "I can't see much disturbed, look at the display case, all the jewellery, it's all still there."

They moved away from the door to let the coroner deal with the body. Henry felt a touch of sadness when the body bag and stretcher went by. He stopped the coroner and asked, "She called me at 10, it must have happened shortly after. Do you think she died instantly?"

"I'll know more once I do the autopsy," said Dr. Carlisle. "But I'd say no, she didn't die on impact, but shortly after. But whoever did this didn't call for help at any rate."

"Bastards," said Henry.

"This is going to be bad for prints, boss," said Travers. "There's stuff everywhere and it's a store, tons of customers pawing everything."

"Concentrate on the door, the cash register, and the glass display case where she hit her head, that'll do us for a start," organized Stafford. "Everything happened in less than thirty minutes. Time for him or her to enter, interact with Mary and kill her, not much else."

They went back in once they received the clearance.

"She did tell me about a small weapon missing," said Henry. "The gun was already gone by the time this second event occurred. It looks like the pads for sales records are missing."

"Unless we find them somewhere else," said Jones. "You can see where they were from the mark in the dust."

"Why would anyone steal only the sales books?" wondered Travers.

"Good question," said Henry. "Let's take the black book, the customer lists and the agenda. It might help us pinpoint the comings and goings. I have the wallet for identification."

"I need to find a next-of-kin, my favourite part of the job," said Henry sarcastically. He walked to his car shaking his head. The driver's licence showed the home address on King Street here in Chesterville. He wondered if she lived alone or if anyone would be at home. He had to be quick. In a small town something like this would spread quickly.

Henry pulled in front of the King Street red brick home and tapped the old fashion door knocker. It took a few minutes and a woman answered. She resembled Mary, only a bit older, with greyish hair. Her outfit was modern and minus all the bangles Mary used to wear.

"Hello, I'm Detective Sergeant Stafford, is this the residence of Mary Blake?" and he showed his badge.

"Yes, I'm her sister Joan. Is anything the matter?" she was nervous but opened the door wider.

"Perhaps it would be better if I could speak to you inside," said Henry. "There's been an accident."

Joan led him into the sitting area to the right. The room was warm and comfortable, decorated to suit the style and the period of the home. Exactly what Harry would expect from an antique dealer. Joan offered him a seat and sat opposite him, looking into his eyes for an explanation.

"There's been an incident at the store," started Henry. "We are just starting our investigation, but it looks like someone pushed Mary and that she fell and hit her head…"

"Is she in the hospital? I can go and see her?" said Joan shaking and rubbing her hands together.

"I'm afraid Mary is dead, I'm so sorry," said Henry. He reached out and placed his hand on her arm.

Joan pushed his hand away and stood up, "It can't be, it can't be…she just left here this morning. She was fine and so happy."

"Is there someone you want me to call, to come and stay with you for a while?" asked Henry.

"No, yes…I have family, I need to call them," she said as tears streamed down her cheeks. "What happens next? The store?"

"We have a policeman on the premises for now. We…I…will stay in touch with you to let you know about the investigation, any questions we may have and how to proceed."

"Thank you," Joan said looking lost and frail. "I'm home most of the time."

At the door, Henry turned and said "I knew Mary, I came into her shop, and she was nice to me. Again, I'm sorry for your loss." Henry went back to the station, he hated Mondays.

Reclining back in his swivel chair Henry realized how little he knew of the woman he had been having casual sex with for the last few months. But then, he thought, that was the nature of "casual" not a relationship, no entanglement. In a broader spectrum, he looked around the office and it registered that he didn't know much about anyone. Not even the people he spent the most time with. Patrick Jones was married and expecting a baby in a couple of months, that he knew. Randy Travers was single, but Henry had never been to his place. "Tell me about your life" had never been a conversation starter for Henry nor had anyone else ever enquired about him in that fashion. Henry made a note to get back in touch with his sister. He might need a next-of-kin one of these days.

Jones and Travers were back and doing what needed to be done to open this case. They started a timeline, bagged and tagged evidence and looked for potential witnesses and anyone to interview. With the material they had, the agenda and the customer list, Henry knew his name would show up. He couldn't help it, so to eliminate awkward glances and questions, he decided to talk to the boss.

Staff Sergeant Glenn was at his desk but on the phone when Henry peered around the door. Glenn was in his fifties, tall and broad-shouldered, the stereotypical police officer. Only the greying hair and the thickening at the waist betrayed the long years behind a desk. Glenn waved him in as he hung up the phone.

"What's up, Stafford? Got yourself a bit of work this morning?" asked Glenn.

"Yes, sir. We're diving into it just now," said Henry. "I need to talk to you about the victim, I knew her."

"Small town, everyone knows everyone else, it happens," said Glenn.

"No, it's a bit more than that. I was a customer, I used to buy vintage portraits from her and…"

"And what? Come out with it Stafford."

"We had a casual acquaintance, some might call it an affair, but you know…," said Henry. "I don't want things to come out later, as we get into the case. Just wanted to be upfront."

"Do you want off the investigation?" asked Glenn. "Will this relationship impact your work?"

"No, I would like to solve this."

"Ok. You're good to go, for now, I appreciate you telling me Stafford."

"One more thing. Can we keep DC Travers a while longer?" asked Henry. "This murder has thrown a lot of work our way."

"I'll see what I can do," replied Glenn. "Since this is a homicide, headquarters is sending a lead detective inspector. The criminal investigation bureau always takes over, but he will work with you."

"Do you know who they are sending?" enquired Stafford.

"Detective Inspector Richard Rowley," said Glenn. "But he goes by Dick for short, his background is British."

"Are you kidding me? Dick?" said Stafford.

"The homicide section is swamped," added Glenn. "Rowley is all they've got. He should be here later today. And by the way…he's retiring in a few weeks."

"Great," murmured Stafford going back to his desk.

The small office was a hive of activity. Henry took his mug and glanced over at the coffee pot.

"Christ, this isn't going to work guys," yelled Henry. They all looked up at him. He never yelled and never lost his cool. But now, of course, they realized it was about coffee.

"If there is one rule, one rule above all others, what is it? Henry asked as he glanced at his audience.

"Whoever takes the last cup, makes a new pot," they all sang in unison. Travers got water and Jones replaced the filter…

"We need to talk to the neighbours and see if anyone saw anything at the time. Staff Sergeant Glenn will handle the media. He'll put something on Crime Stoppers," said Henry.

Travers put the pot down and made for the door, "I'm on it."

"The local paper already called and I told her we would put out a statement at the end of the day," said Jones and Henry nodded.

Jones was looking at the black book. It contained a list of customers, regulars he thought. They had phone numbers and some had stars beside their names.

"Hey, Henry. You said you shopped there, will your name be in this book?" asked Jones, flipping over to the "S" in the book.

Henry thought he would be since Mary knew how to contact him when she held items in reserve for him, but he didn't say anything.

"There are some names with stars beside them. Do you know what it means?" asked Jones. He noticed one or two with a small note "never again" and a few with one or two stars. By the time he flipped over to "S" he realized Stafford had three stars.

Henry didn't want to give more information than necessary about his relationship with the victim but he had a good idea what the star system was all about.

"You must be something special, boss," laughed Jones. "You have three stars! I'll start interviewing anyone who was on the agenda for this week. I'll cross-reference with the customers in the black book."

Lovely, thought Henry as he finally filled his coffee cup to the rim. This occasion called for black. "First thing tomorrow I'll go back and talk to the sister. I'll be in after that."

Staff Sergeant Glenn walked out of his office accompanied by an older man.

"Gather around everybody," said Glenn. "This is Detective Inspector Richard Rowley, from CIB. He'll be the lead investigator for this homicide."

DI Rowley was short, stocky with thinning grey hair. He nodded to everyone. Glenn directed him to an empty desk next to Stafford's. Glenn introduced them.

"DS Stafford has a good grasp of what is involved, of course being local it helps," said Glenn. "He'll help you with anything you need."

"Hi Stafford, you can call me Dick," said Rowley. "What do you have so far?"

Henry showed him a file he had started, and the timeline, and explained what had been done so far.

"Excellent," said Rowley. "So, this is an interesting one, isn't it?"

"We're looking for witnesses right now, and Jones is going through her agenda and customer lists," added Stafford. "Would you like to see any of it?"

"Yes, no, I see," said Rowley. "An interesting one for sure. I think you have everything in order. Well started, Stafford."

"Ok, then," said Stafford. "First thing tomorrow morning I will be seeing the sister again. Do you want me to pick you up here before I go?"

"No, no, I think you have all of this well in hand Stafford," said Rowley. "I'll stay here and just be available if I'm ever needed. Now I'll just go and unpack."

"Sure, thank you, Dick."

Chapter 5

Out of habit, Henry threw a few chicken breasts on the grill and a pot of potatoes to boil on the side burner. He could always use the chicken for sandwiches and make potato salad. It would be good for a few days if he didn't feel like cooking.

The smell of light smoke combined with the searing meat and barbecue sauce, drew Jeremy over.

"Wow, that smells good," said Jeremy watching Henry turn the chicken and brush on more sauce.

"It's the sauce. I make my own," said Henry. "Want a piece?"

"I had dinner, but a small piece to try it, please. You barbecue a lot, do you also go camping and hunt and fish?" asked the young man.

Henry laughed, "No, just the grilling, it's easy and it's survival."

Noticing that Henry didn't make a plate for himself, Jeremy added "Not hungry, hard day?"

"How did you know?" asked Henry.

"I see it with Mom when she has hard days in the emergency room. I guess it must be the same for you with police work."

"It probably is," said Henry. "We had something happen today and it is someone I knew; you'll probably see it in the papers."

"Did you always want to be a policeman," said Jeremy running his last bite of chicken over the sauce left on his plate.

"No, I didn't know what I wanted to do, at your age. A friend said he was going for an interview for police work and I followed him. A few tests later, there I was, in uniform."

"Do you like it though? Do you wish you had done something else?" Jeremy's curiosity getting the better of him. At fourteen there was already discussion at school about career paths and orientation. He was curious to see how other people made their choices.

"Yes, I do enjoy it, mostly when there's nothing to do," Henry laughed. "When there are problems, you see the bad side of things, like your mother must do in her work. Yet, when you help someone, it feels good. Otherwise, I'm not sure what I would have done, probably the trades."

"Like professional boat builder," laughed Jeremy.

"You're cheeky, aren't you?" smirked Henry. "My problem was that I was good at a whole bunch of things, but passionate about nothing. It all seemed even to me, that every line of work had good and bad. As far as earning a living, police work had good pay, benefits, and pension and it was easy enough for me to get in."

Henry picked up the chicken and potatoes and turned off the grill. "I'm not doing any computer stuff tonight, but if you have time another day, we can work on it."

"Sure, I have a friend who can loan me a game, maybe we can try that," closed Jeremy.

For the rest of the evening, Henry went over the day's events and tried to make some order out of them. Whoever went into the shop and killed Mary, what were they after? What could she have that was worth her life, wondered Henry. When he finally fell asleep, he had nightmares. He woke up early feeling more wrinkled than his shirt if that was possible. He showered and looked around for something to throw on that wasn't from the '70s with crease marks. Perhaps it was time he renewed his wardrobe. Sitting in the doorway, both KC and Oscar meowed, either agreeing to him getting new clothes or looking for breakfast.

As he drove on King Street, Henry couldn't help but admire the red-brick home that held so much character. The arched windows on the third floor, the wrap-around veranda and the bay window. All were much more impressive than his sixties bungalow. Joan Blake was expecting him. She also looked tired with lines and dark circles under her eyes. She led him to the kitchen.

"Would you like a coffee, Mr Stafford?" she asked.

"That would be nice, thank you. Are you managing alright?"

"Yes, it's difficult, with this all being so sudden, but we're muddling through," Joan said. "They have been in touch with us, about releasing the body, so we can make funeral arrangements."

"That's good," continued Henry. "I need to ask you a few more questions. We are trying to find out what happened and more importantly why… Should I call you Miss Blake or Mrs…"

"Joan will be fine. I was Miss Blake, then Mrs Andrews, but I'm still Joan."

"Good. Your sister Mary was divorced, any children?"

"Divorced, yes, a long time ago, no children. It was a friendly enough parting. Her husband George McDonald moved to Nova Scotia, soon after the divorce. We don't hear from him."

"Did Mary mention anything lately, about a customer being difficult or harassing her?" asked Henry.

Joan was lost in her thoughts for a while and replied, "Yes, there was this Russell fellow. He called her a few times, but recently she had mentioned him watching her from across the street and he approached her when she closed the store."

"Do you have his full name?"

"Russell Davis, I believe. She mentioned it to me because I work in the shop, a couple of days a week when Mary takes, sorry, took days off or went to an auction or an estate sale."

"I see, so you were familiar with the routine of the shop," added Henry. He scribbled a few notes in his book. "Did she seem scared of this Russell Davis?

"No, she didn't seem particularly worried," said Joan. "Mary was popular with men, but she didn't want anything serious. She brushed a few off over time."

"Did you notice anything out of the ordinary, anything special or rare, of more value than the usual items?"

"No, some pieces are better than others, but you've seen the shop. Mary had regular customers from Ottawa and even Montreal, who knew she had a flair for good antiques. It did well enough to bring an income for her to live off, but it's no gold mine."

"Did you know that Mary had a gun and that it went missing?" asked Henry.

"Yes, I know about the gun, it's kept locked in a metal box behind the counter. But I didn't know it went missing."

"Yes, she reported it on Monday morning, she noticed it was gone when she opened the store," said Henry. "But she wasn't certain when it went missing."

"It's not something I touched; I was scared of it. Joan hesitated and looked away from Henry before adding, "She never told me why she had it, or even how she got it."

"Thank you for this, I might contact you again if I have more questions," said Henry.

"The shop is closed now, but I plan to keep it open, for a while anyway, then I'll see," said Joan.

"Do let me know when the funeral will be if you don't mind," said Henry as he placed his business card on the table.

Henry drove the country roads back to the station, feeling baffled. He would get Jones to investigate Russell Davis. To him, this case had the feel of something that would end up in a box, filed with other unsolved cases, years later to be moved to the cold cases storage depot. Henry leaned heavily on the law of averages. God, he was the poster child for it. But this time, he just couldn't accept it, there must be something, someone to take to account.

Before even going to his desk, Henry stopped by the coffee maker, filled his mug and added a touch of milk. He spun around in his swivel chair, took a sip and nearly choked on it. For the love of God, who in their right mind, had made a pot of Vanilla Hazelnut flavoured coffee? That was an aberration and an insult to coffee beans the world over!

Travers smiled and said, "Vanilla Hazelnut, the new girlfriend gave me a pouch to try. Like it?"

Henry should have known it was Travers, "No, I hate it…coffee doesn't need to be 'flavoured.' It already has a flavour and it's called 'coffee'…" Henry turned around to switch on his computer when he saw a bunch of little paper stars all over his keyboard. The guys looked at him and laughed.

Jones giggled, "I started the interviews from the customer book, I did a few with stars and figured out what it means…Woot Woot, the boss has three stars. Way to go, boss!"

Henry figured he was too old to blush, and between the stars and the vanilla coffee, his day was off to a less-than-stellar start. "Back to work, guys. Travers, make a decent pot of coffee, will you."

Noticing the empty desk beside him, Henry asked "Does anyone know where DI Rowley is?"

"Yes," said Jones. "He's at the bowling alley."

"What?" asked Stafford a bit confused.

"The bowling alley," repeated Jones. "It seems he's a competitive bowler, so he wanted to check out our facilities."

"So, Dick is a bowler," murmured Stafford.

On Friday, Henry dressed for a funeral. He went to work first to see if there was any progress with the interviews. Jones was also wearing his best jacket and would be coming along to the service. Attending a funeral served two purposes, connecting with the victim's family and seeing if anything is out of sorts. One could notice an unexpected attendee or tense interaction between family members. Jones was plugging away on his computer when Henry arrived.

"I ran a check for Mary Blake and other members of the family, to see if anyone had a record," said Jones.

"And? Anything?" asked Henry.

"Two things, a domestic disturbance, six years ago and some minor infractions for Alexander McNeill, a nephew," said Jones.

"We can look at bringing Alexander in after we attend the service. Coming? Is DI Rowley in this morning?" asked Stafford.

"Yes, he did come in, but now he's out," said Jones, trying very hard not to smile. "He's gone to the hardware store; they have a sale on. He said he had complete confidence in you."

Stafford and Jones slid into the back row pew, unnoticed amongst the many who had come for the service. Mary Blake was well-regarded in the community, with many being friends and customers.

An older man, sitting with Joan Blake could be the father. Sitting with them was a couple with their teenage son. The priest interacted with the attendees and he reflected a long-term knowledge of the Blake family. Henry noticed a few people he had encountered when he visited the shop. Glancing around he wondered how many had been on that regular customers' list and if any were guilty of assaulting her.

The funeral procession went to the cemetery, and after a few words there, condolences were presented to the family. Stafford and Jones lined up, shook hands and added the conventional "I'm sorry for your loss." Henry felt that the family was still in shock. Everything had happened so quickly.

"Did you notice that young man? Alexander McNeill" said Jones. "It's the kid from the mug shot. The one with a record, the attempted burglary, loitering, and general pain the neck teenage angst stuff."

"It does ring a bell with the young man that was shot, the nurse had said his name was Alex, about 19 years old. He did seem a little fidgety when I shook his hand," said Henry. "Let's bring him in and call the nurse in to see if she can identify him."

"Do you want me to wait or get him today?" asked Jones.

"I don't think he's a risk of running out of town, or suspects we know anything," explained Henry. "Given what the family is going through right now, let's bring him in on Monday."

"There is this other guy though, that Joan Blake mentioned," said Henry. "Russell Davis alleged to have called and stalked Mary a few times, waiting for her at store closing and the likes."

"I will check and see if he's in the book of customers," said Jones. "That should speed things up if we have an address." Jones retrieved the little black book and flipped through the pages.

"He's there, but no stars," laughed Jones. "It says he's in Cornwall. I'll track him down and take Travers with me for a surprise visit."

"Good, that's one lead, at least," said Henry despondently.

Chapter 6

Henry who loved nothing more than to leave the office behind as soon as the clock showed five o'clock on a Friday, found it difficult now. This case was going nowhere fast and it was more than he ever wanted. There were always going to be too many people milling around that antique shop. Too many customers, buyers and sellers, with trivia that didn't amount to much. No proof of anything of value was taken to claim a motive for burglary. Interviews of people in a little black book that was again another dead end. The only person the neighbours had seen going in was him.

On his way home Henry stopped to get beer and hamburger buns. He had invited the guys over for a barbecue. He thought a casual get-together might relax the tensions brought on by this unusual workload. He was warming up the grill when Jeremy came over.

"Do you want to stay for dinner?" asked Henry. "I have the guys from work coming, you are welcome to stay. You can bring Ellie over for a hot dog if it's ok with your mother. And she can also pick up something if she wants."

"Thanks, I'll stay but Ellie is gone with her father for the weekend," said Jeremy.

"And you don't go with them?" He was unsure of their family structure but he didn't think Jeremy and Ellie had the same father.

"No, he's not my father and he doesn't want me around," said Jeremy. "That's why my mother and he broke up. Need any help?"

"Sure, how about you get some extra chairs out of the garage? We might be seven or eight if Travers and Jones bring their partners."

Henry was very new at this entertaining business, but he counted on the food to hold everything together. This would be a very casual and relaxed gathering; the evening was warm. He might just ace this!

Henry had asked DI Rowley, but it was the weekend of his bowling tournament, so he politely declined. Travers arrived first, minus the new girlfriend. Nothing unusual there, Randy made his way through strings of girlfriends like beads on a rosary. He had brought a six-pack with him and a large pack of napkins as his contribution. He was in his late twenties, well-built with that bad boy look that women liked. Henry never understood why a lot of women liked that sort of man, a challenge, a project. A turn-key sort of man like himself didn't draw much attention.

Patrick Jones and his wife Judy followed soon after. Judy was seven months pregnant and Henry thought she looked wonderful. He had also invited Paul Larose and Justin Bates, two of his new IT buddies.

The food was great, they talked about everything but the case. Jeremy was introduced as a friend and neighbour and found himself deep in conversation with the two computer geeks. When Lisa dropped by, Jones recognized her from the hospital interview. He didn't want to spoil the party, so he didn't mention anything about her needing to come in to identify Alex McNeill. Travers was quick to open a chair for her right beside him and next to Judy Jones. Henry noticed and thought Travers was always the charmer.

Jeremy made a plea for a beer, as always. His mother said no, but Travers waded in, "Oh, come on let him have a small glass. He's going to taste it anyway if he's curious. Better with a bunch of cops than with hoodlums in a public park!"

"Yes, must better with us, hoodlums in a back yard…," laughed Jones.

"Oh, ok, but just a small glass," conceded Lisa.

Jeremy grinned, finally he thought…then he took a sip and realized he didn't like the taste of beer one bit. They all laughed at the face he made.

Henry was pleased with himself. It had all gone well and the evening had taken his mind off the case. He said goodbye to everyone and Jeremy offered to stay and help clean up, and so did Lisa.

"Are you busy tomorrow?" Henry asked Jeremy. "Can you come with me shopping in Ottawa, if it's good with your mother?"

Lisa nodded and Jeremy asked what time he should come over.

"Is morning good with you, or do you need time to sleep off that beer you had?"

"Morning is fine," said Jeremy.

Henry hadn't told Jeremy what the shopping trip was all about. He wanted to get new clothes and thought of getting a second opinion to support his choices. Someone younger might have a better perspective. His own taste was not to be trusted.

Mid-morning Jeremy jumped in the car ready for an adventure. "What are we going shopping for? You didn't say yesterday."

"Clothes and perhaps we can grab lunch while we are out," replied Henry.

"Oh, you should have asked my mother to come, she's good with clothes."

"No, it might expedite things if it's just the two of us," said Henry. Jeremy felt flattered by the trust and the influence he was now wielding.

"Are you getting jeans? You never wear jeans, and everyone has them now," opened Jeremy.

"I don't know, work pants probably. I don't think I like jeans; they don't seem to fit me right. I always end up looking like Elmer Fudd."

"That's because you need to go to a proper jeans store, not buy them at K-Mart or Woolworth's," coached Jeremy. "A real jeans store will have different models, so they fit you just right."

"See that's why I'm bringing you along," laughed Henry.

The two of them had a good morning and went for pizza at lunchtime. Henry walked away with a few pairs of work pants, jeans and shirts. He bought

Jeremy a T-shirt, something he said his friends would envy, from a rock band Henry didn't know. When they arrived home, Jeremy showed his mother the t-shirt and she offered to pay Henry back. He wouldn't hear of it and she thanked him. Lisa could see the two of them had an enjoyable time and she was glad for it. Jeremy's father was nowhere to be found, and she didn't have family close by. As for Ellie's father, he had been accepting of the boy at first, but when his daughter came along, he rejected Jeremy. As a single mother, she did her best, but there were things a teenage boy dealt with that left her baffled.

Henry opted to clean his closet and wondered what he would do with Paula's clothes. He packed everything of hers in boxes. Funny enough, or so he thought, as he folded each piece, he couldn't remember her wearing any of it. Every recollection he had of Paula was in sepia or black and white. He didn't remember what she wore, but he remembered her voice. Every so often she would drop into the police station and ask to see him. She would tell him the car was empty and expect him to go next door and fill it up. He would pay for it, saving her spending money for lunch with the girls or whatever it was she did with her days since she didn't work outside the home.

The lingerie drawer was another bust, the content reminded him of packing up his grandmother's personal items after she passed. Flannel buttoned-up nightgowns, baggy underwear, nothing there to fan the flames of desire. Henry imagined his own boxer shorts generated the same comments at her end. Then underneath all this cotton, was a black lace set he'd never seen before. He was sure he'd remember that…it was reserved for next-door neighbour Edgar! He wondered whether he should get a new bed. He taped all the boxes and took them to the basement. If she didn't ask for anything back within a month, off to the Salvation Army it would go.

In the evening he relaxed working on his new box of photos. Of course, that led directly to wondering about the case and Mary's murder. As a motive, robbery was a line of enquiry that was leading nowhere. Thinking of motives, Henry knew that robbery, jealousy and revenge were the standard set. This murder was not random, but how targeted was it, or even premeditated? She was pushed, hit her head and left to die. The result of a heated argument?

The only person that anyone saw around the shop that Monday morning was Henry. Murder 101 was all about Means, Motives and Opportunity. Henry now had the uneasy feeling that this line of thinking would propel him right to the top of the list for suspects.

Chapter 7

The press, following the same train of thought, was quick to highlight the fact that the leading detective in the Mary Blake murder case, had a relationship with the victim. DS Henry Stafford was a client who had an affair with the deceased and was the last person to speak to her. He was also the first on the scene and the one to call the station. The reporter was creating links and motives that were embarrassing. The Monday morning edition was dropped on Henry's desk with a copy to Staff Sergeant Glenn.

Henry was now dreading Monday mornings, strong coffee or not. He opted to wear the new pants but put on an old shirt. The guys would tease him if he showed up with a whole new outfit. The only time Henry looked at himself in the mirror was when he shaved. Otherwise, he didn't think of himself at all, never glanced at a reflection wondering if he looked good enough. But now, his grey eyes looked tired, even this early in the morning. He had the unpleasant feeling that his position on the Happiness Train was precarious.

Before he could even go to his desk, his name was called and told that Staff Sergeant Glenn was looking for him. Nothing good ever came of an audience with the boss on a Monday morning. Staff Sergeant Glenn was glancing at his copy of the newspaper when he ushered Henry to his office. DI Rowley was sitting in front of the desk.

"I'm afraid this is not a good look for us, the investigating police force," said Glenn. "I will have to remove you from the Mary Blake investigation. Jones will be the lead for now."

"I understand how it looks, but you know I have nothing to do with her murder," said Henry.

"Of course, I do," said Glenn. "I've known you for over ten years and if nothing else, I would credit you with enough brains not to set it up that way, if you did."

"Yes, I agree with this decision," said DI Rowley. "It's an interesting one, isn't it? I trust Staff Sergeant Glenn knows what's best."

"Can I stay on the Alex McNeill gunshot enquiry?" asked Henry. "I don't see it as being directly related to the murder of his aunt."

"No, yes, you can continue with that, brilliant," said Rowley glancing at Glenn.

"I need all my people working anyway," said Glenn.

"What's next?" asked Stafford.

"You'll be questioned of course. But not by us, internal affairs will send someone from another detachment, headquarters. I'll let you know when they want to talk to you."

"Thank you," said Henry. "In the meantime, I'll stay away from the press."

Henry went back to work and threw the newspaper that was on his desk in the garbage can. He filled his mug with black coffee and walked right past the doughnuts, that's how dire things were. He called for a uniform constable to bring Alexander McNeill in for an interview and arranged for Lisa Stuart to come in for identification of the suspect.

"Hey Travers, do we have the report of the fingerprints from the metal case that held the gun?" asked Henry. "I imagined we lifted the prints off it, is the case in the evidence room?"

"Yes, to both questions, boss. The prints were those of Mary Blake as expected and others from Alexander McNeill. Not very smart of him not to use gloves if he was going to lift the gun," concluded Travers.

Henry took the report from Travers and went to the evidence room to look at the metal case. The lock was not damaged so it must have been picked or the thief had the key. The grey box had a foam insert cut out to hold the handgun and a magazine. The shape in the foam reminded Henry of a Smith & Wesson, a 539 but he couldn't be certain. He wondered where Mary had obtained such a weapon, but in her world of trading, it wouldn't be that difficult. He moved the foam and found a folded piece of paper underneath. He doubted the gun came with a warranty or instructions; he was intrigued. He took the paper back to his desk.

When nurse Lisa Stuart came into the police station to identify the suspect, DS Stafford was talking with his partners. Lisa glanced at his backside in its new pants and noted the marked improvements over the first time they had met. He was still wearing a wrinkled mismatched shirt and tie, but the train of progress had left the station. Henry put on his jacket, smiled and told her about the identification process.

"There's no need to worry, you will see him but he won't see you," explained Henry. "He will not be told who identified him."

Lisa followed Henry to the interview room, they stood behind a glass that allowed Lisa to look at a young man. He was sitting, fidgeting nervously.

"Is this the man you treated for a bullet wound, at the emergency room of the Winchester Hospital, on Sunday, May 12?" asked Henry.

"Yes, it is him."

"Thanks, Lisa. Thank you for coming in," said Henry. Were you working last night? I hope we didn't upset your schedule."

"No, it's fine. It was a day off. Henry, I'm sorry about this but Jeremy saw the newspaper this morning. He was upset about it and had some questions."

"Oh, I'll have a chat with him," said Henry embarrassed. "I hope you can trust me; the article is not painting a true picture."

"I couldn't say much about it, because I don't know, but if it comes from you, it would be better," said Lisa.

"I will, thank you for letting me know."

Stafford and Jones opted to question Alex McNeill together since there was a link between the gun and the murder victim. It was a small lead, but the only one they had so far. Stafford knew that his boss's orders were clear – no involvement with the murder case, but here he was. The detective reasoned that he had no choice. Having separate interviews with McNeill, one about the gun and one about the murder, would be ludicrous. Abbott and Costello knew that they could work better together to pry information from McNeill.

"Abbott and Costello, here we go," said Jones. "Do you know that's what the guys call us, behind our backs?"

"Yes, I know…but I've been called worse by better people," replied Stafford. They entered the interview room each carrying a file folder.

"Good day, Mr McNeill. I'm Detective Sergeant Henry Stafford and this is Detective Constable Patrick Jones. Thank you for helping us with our investigation."

"Why'd you arrest me, I didn't do anything," started Alex. The young man had a cocky, defiant look about him.

"We didn't arrest you," said Stafford. "We just have a few questions, that's all."

He continued, "On the evening of Sunday, May 12, did you go to the emergency room of the Winchester Hospital?"

"Nope, was nowhere near, that place. I was out with friends, walking in the park, it was just after the Sunday evening Church service," smirked Alex.

"Plenty of witnesses at the evening service, I go there myself all the time. It's convenient and doesn't cut into my morning," smiled Stafford. "Of course, the only evening service in this area is at St. Mary's in Chesterville and on Saturdays…This might be a moot point, but it's Catholic and you're United. So, before we waste any more time, I'll tell you someone identified you, at the hospital, with a bullet wound, on Sunday evening."

"Care to go over your Sunday evening again?" prompted Stafford.

"My mistake, I had the wrong Sunday," smiled Alex, self-assurance still there but slowly shaking the foundations. "I was shot, it's not a crime. It's quite the reverse, I was a victim!"

"So, you're here now to report a crime?" asked Stafford. "Let me take this down? You didn't report it while you were in the emergency room though. Preferred to walk out with a few supplies instead? Can we go over how it happened, who shot you?"

"I don't know, I was walking downtown, a car went by, and then I had this pain in my side," said Alex. "I had a look and I was bleeding, walked myself to the hospital."

"Did you notice the car? Make, model?"

"No, I didn't see a thing," said Alex still smiling.

"Didn't have a peek at the driver, the back seat, the window must have been rolled down?"

"It came from behind, didn't see a thing," confirmed Alex.

"Ok, I see where this is going," said Stafford. "What do you think Jones? I see Wile E Cayote as the driver myself…"

"For sure, not something the Roadrunner would do," said Jones shaking his head.

"Listen, kid, I'm getting older by the minute and I have better things to do, my coffee is getting cold and I hate that," said Stafford.

"And you shouldn't mess with DS Stafford on low caffeine, so stop the bullshit," said Jones.

"We have your aunt deceased, her handgun is reported missing, and your fingerprints are on the box. A total coincidence we have you showing up at the hospital with a bullet wound. Imagine that..." adds Jones.

At the mention of his aunt, Alex lost his smile and he lowered his head.

"We know you have a record; it's not going to be good for your future to add anything to it," said Stafford. "Best if you tell us what you know and at least save your hide in this bad situation."

"Yes, I went to the hospital, but I didn't want to report anything because of the record and my father," said Alex. "I have more to worry about if he finds out."

"Who shot you?" asked Stafford. He could see the wheels turning in Alex's head. Stafford expected to be entertained a while longer.

"I shot myself," said Alex. "You see, I borrowed the gun from my aunt's store, to clean it. Then the shot went off and I got hit. That's the whole story."

"Winchester is a pretty quiet town, not much going on downtown on a Sunday night," said Stafford. "But of all the coincidences, we happen to have a reported stolen car, later found with a bullet in its trunk, and right on Main Street. Imagine that."

"It'd be a waste of our time to try and find other people to pin this on when we have you, Alex McNeill, connected to it all. Might as well point everything to you and go for coffee, what do you think boss?" said Jones.

"My thinking exactly, do you want to write it up?" asked Stafford.

"Wait a minute, I'm the victim here, I told you, you can't charge me with anything?" yelled Alex.

"Stolen property from the hospital, a stolen weapon from a murdered storekeeper, fingerprints on the gun case," rambles Jones. "A good start for me."

Alex was quick to realize he painted himself into a corner. He doesn't have the composure to lie anymore, he's shaking.

"Ok, Ok. I borrowed the gun from my aunt's store. I was going to return it. It was just to show the guys. You know, showing off," said Alex. "I told a few friends I could get a gun, and I did. On that Sunday night, we went to the park and got drunk, one of the guys said we should steal a car and joyride around town. We stopped on Main Street and joked about breaking into a store. They wanted me to show them the gun, and Murphy was playing with it when it went off."

"Do you have the names of your friends?" asked Stafford. "We'll find out anyway, you might as well spread out the shit you're in now."

"Jerry Murphy and Mike Smith," said Alex. Jones jotted down the names.

"Can you tell me about the car, colour, make?" asked Stafford.

"A black Chevy Caprice, a newer one. I was at the back of the car, joking around and the bullet went through me into the trunk. When Murphy realized what he'd done, they drove me to the hospital. They took off and left the car in some parking lot off Main."

"Let's go back to the gun," said Jones. "When did you steal it from your aunt?"

"A few days before the joy ride," said Alex. "I help at the antique shop occasionally, moving things around, loading the bigger pieces. I took it and I thought I would just bring it back after I showed it to the guys."

"Do you have keys to the store?" asked Jones. "And does anyone else to your knowledge?"

"Yes, keys are easy enough to come by," explained Alex. "Aunt Mary leaves them out by the cash register and Aunt Joan also has a set. I heard about the gun when Mary and Joan were talking about it."

"And where is the gun now?" asked Stafford. The weapon had not shown up anywhere in the vicinity so far.

"Jerry had it last, I think he threw it away in the back of the parking lot where they left the car."

"That's it for now, you are free to go," said Stafford. "We will look into all of this, but you can expect to hear from us again." Stafford and Jones collected their files and stood up to leave. Alex

McNeill now looked terrified; he didn't make a move to leave the safety of the interview room.

"You won't tell my father, will you?" he asked.

"Not at this time, there is no need, but I would come clean if I were you," said Stafford. "If charges are laid later, he will find out." Alex shook his head and walked out of the room.

Stafford and Jones discussed the interview and planned to go forward with questioning the friends. They could decide on laying charges afterwards. Both came to the same conclusion, that Alex had lied about where the gun was. Henry also felt uneasy about how scared the boy had been about his father finding out. He sensed it to be more than the expected disappointment from a father towards a son and its consequences. It came across as a raw physical fear.

"Jones, do you want to call William Campbell, the owner of the stolen car and see if he wants to press charges?" asked Henry.

Henry poured his coffee and grabbed a muffin. Travers' new girlfriend had baked healthy snacks for them. As expected for a "healthy" snack, it tasted like cardboard. Henry threw the muffin into the bin; it dropped to the bottom like a rock. He reached back for a chocolate-dipped doughnut. As he did, he realized how much of a cliché he was. The stereotypical cops and doughnuts, but…these were from the neighbourhood bakery. Here in Winchester, there was no big-name franchised doughnut shop, no drive-thru, no mass production. Only homemade-style goodness from the smell-good place on Main Street. He might not die healthy but at least he would shoot for contentment again.

He picked up the piece of paper he had found in the gun case earlier. It read "Keep this in case you need it. If I hold on to it, I might use it" and it was signed simply "E." Henry cursed, yet another mystery to add to all the unsolved issues they had to deal with.

Chapter 8

Henry was officially off the murder case but that didn't stop him from taking a risk and dropping in at *Treasures to Share*. His curiosity got the better of him. Whether his line of enquiry would prove useful, only time would tell. The shop was still officially closed but Joan had told him she would be there. There was a commotion at the back door, two guys from the junk removal company were wrestling with a large sofa. The item was wedged at the back door, unwilling to leave the premises.

By definition the piece of furniture was too large to be called a love seat...function over definition, it was only semantics. Nostalgia washed over Henry, quickly replaced by a wave of horror when he pictured the heavy traffic it had supported over the years. Henry wondered whether the sofa was headed for the landfill or a forensics lab to be used as a teaching aid. One thing was clear though, the discount days were over.

Joan Blake was in the back office straightening up. It was an opportune moment to see if there was more to be found here.

"Hi, Joan. You're busy, I see," opened Henry.

"Yes, I'm planning to open up again at the end of the week and there was much cleaning up to do," Joan said. Her eyes watered, at the idea of the blood-soaked floor in the front.

"I have a few questions again if you don't mind," began Henry. "It's a nice shop, how did Mary come to acquire it?"

"Our mother passed away about ten years ago, there was a bit of money that went to my father of course. But he wanted to share it with the three children right away, rather than wait until he passed. He thought it helped more that way."

"That was nice of him," said Henry. "So, Mary started the shop, does she own the building?"

"Yes, she also had a bit of money herself, from the divorce. She bought the building from our brother-in-law, Hugh McNeill. He's in real estate and owned the place at the time."

"Would he be Alex's father then?" asked Henry.

"Yes. He is married to our younger sister Evelyn and they live in Winchester," explained Joan.

"Who has keys, aside from you and Mary?"

"Only the two of us. Mary had the locks changed when she bought the place."

"Hugh and his family, wouldn't have keys?"

"Oh, no, she wouldn't want that…I mean, there was no need to," said Joan. Did Henry pick up a note of fear on that last comment? The image of the letter he'd found in the gun case flashed before his eyes, the signature "E" and Hugh McNeill's wife was Evelyn.

Henry threw a bait, "Were there any issues with the deal? Buyer's remorse? Sometimes things happen when you deal with family."

"No, no, Evelyn and Mary were very close, we all are really," said Joan. "But Hugh can be a little overbearing sometimes but Mary would have none of that."

"Thanks again, Joan. I look forward to the shop re-opening. I wish you good luck."

Since Henry couldn't be directly involved in the murder investigation, he would concentrate on young Alexander and investigate the McNeill family dynamics. That seemed intriguing to him. Plus, he had a three o'clock rendezvous with internal affairs and his interrogation to look forward to. The weekend would be bliss!

Staff Sergeant Gerry Doucette and Staff Sergeant Rémi Lafrance came directly from the East Region Headquarters in Smith Falls. They were to investigate the involvement and relationship between the murder victim Mary Blake and investigating officer DS Henry Stafford. Henry was as eager as anyone in the force to free himself of any suspicions. He didn't hide anything but he could see how it looked. Everyone introduced themselves and the two officers had already been briefed on the case so far.

"DS Stafford, regarding the victim, Miss Mary Blake, it has come to light that you knew her.

Intimate knowledge, that you were having an affair with her. Can you tell us about this?" asked Lafrance.

"I have known Mary Blake for the last eight years at least. I was a customer at her antique shop," said Stafford.

"And had you been having an affair for all this time?" continued Lafrance.

"No, it began after my wife left me, in November last year," said Henry. "It was very casual. I would see her maybe once a month when I went to Chesterville to browse her shop."

"You were a very esteemed client, according to her star system. In her black book of customers, you ranked three stars," smiled Doucette.

"I'm not sure how that happened, but yes, the investigation did uncover that," said Stafford. Where others saw this as a claim to fame, Henry found only embarrassment.

"On the morning of her death, she phoned you and you went over and discovered the body?" asked Lafrance.

"Yes, she called me at 10 am to say her handgun was missing and she thought it was theft or a break-in. The gun was not registered and that's why she called me first. It is also our jurisdiction," said Stafford. "I found the body and called it in. I also told Staff Sergeant Glenn about my relationship with the deceased straight away."

"Yes, we saw the note on that," said Lafrance. "It was wise of you to point it out. Were you aware that Miss Blake was seeing several other customers, also under her star rating?

"She never told me, but I suspected that if she enjoyed my company, she might also do the same with other customers. I had no reason to assume it was more than it seemed," said Henry.

"And did you get anything in exchange from those encounters?" asked Doucette.

"Yes, it was all part of the negotiations, if you want, a sort of game, a discount in exchange for personal favours," explained Henry, realizing how pathetic that sounded. Would they think he was prostituting himself in exchange for a few dollars off old photos? No…they laughed.

"Nice way to spend a Sunday afternoon, if you can," said Doucette.

"Were you ever angry that the discounts were not enough? Not getting a good return on investment, so to speak?" asked Lafrance.

"Absolutely not," said Henry. "It was a game, we both knew what we were in for, both adults and under no false pretences."

"Did you go in that morning, thinking you would confront her about seeing other customers? Did you want more out of the deal? Got into an argument, pushed her and she fell and hit her head?"

"Good God, NO!" exclaimed Henry, then he calmed down. "Listen, I know how it looks, but I had no emotional investment there. I never called her or tried to see her at any other times but when we discussed an artifact. I was interested in nothing more. She was nice, we had fun together and I was flattered by the attention. That was all."

"For now, you are off the case, and we will monitor the progress, and see who else is coming up as suspect. I would tell you though that it's slim pickings right now. Winchester station is running a murder investigation of a woman in broad daylight, on King Street, with no motives and no suspects. Way to go Winchester!" said Doucette.

Henry was free to go, but he felt no relief or vindication from their line of questioning. He just rolled himself right out of the "Content" car into the "Sad Sack" compartment. He was sliding further and further down on the Happiness Train.

Jones and Travers were on their way to Cornwall, with a location for Russell Davis. He was a security guard at the Cornwall Community Hospital and his day shift ended at 3 pm. Jones wanted the surprise factor and knew that Davis would be available to talk. Whether he'd be willing is another matter, but this way he wouldn't have time to prepare his answers.

They pulled into the parking lot around 2:30 p.m. and made their way to the security office. The supervisor called Davis to the office. Surprise was one way to describe his look when he saw the two police officers. They found a quiet area to talk and introduced themselves. Russell Davis made an odd security guard. He was in his thirties, his hair already thinning. Heavy-set in his case was a diminutive because Davis was large. His belly flopped over his pants, making his belt disappear. Jones thought it was a good thing he worked in a hospital because any amount of physical activity was likely to send him into cardiac arrest.

"Mr Davis are you familiar with Miss Mary Blake?" asked Jones. "She has an antique shop in Chesterville."

"Yes, I've been in there, once or twice, just browsing," said Davis.

"And do you know, she was murdered on Monday, May 20th, shortly after 10 am?" said Travers.

"Yes, I think I read something about that in the papers," said Davis. He seemed relaxed and was not giving anything away.

"Where were you on that Monday morning?" asked Jones.

"Let me think," said Davis. He took out a small blue notebook and looked at his schedule. "I was working nights from Sunday to Monday, so probably at home getting ready for bed."

"Can anyone vouch for that? Spouse?" asked Travers.

"No, I live alone," said Davis. "But I had nothing to do with any of this. I barely know her."

"We have you in her list of customers and sellers, so it was more than just a one-off," added Jones. "We also have information that you had called her several times and even stalked her."

"Stalking is a big word, here," said Davis on the defensive now. "I did try to talk to her, I wanted to discuss something I sold her."

"Did you ever wait for her and approach her when she was closing her shop?" asked Jones.

"Well, that's not a crime is it," added Davis. "I tried to talk to her but she was brushing me off."

"What was the issue? Why did you need to talk to her so badly?" asked Travers.

"I sold her a box of photos, some artefacts and old things from my grandmother's house," said Davis. "She low-balled me on the price, I found out later some of the things were worth a lot more. I was trying to get the items back."

"Did you want some more money?" asked Jones.

"No, I wanted my items back, I asked her to give me the names of the people who bought the stuff, so I could get it back. She wouldn't hear of it and told me off."

"Did you go on that Monday morning, entered the shop and argued with her?" said Travers.

"No, I was nowhere near the place," said Davis, but he looked away from them and rubbed his hands together.

"You know that as a security guard, we have your prints on file. We also lifted prints off the shop," explained Jones. "Is there anything else you wish to tell us before we look into this any further?"

"No, no, I have nothing to say," insisted Davis. "Wasn't there, don't have a clue who was."

"Thank you very much for your time, we'll be in touch if there is anything else. And, by the way, don't leave town. The two officers made their way back to their car.

"So, what do you think?" asked Jones. "Anything strikes you as odd?"

"Yeah, those vending machines, of the waiting room, not a healthy snack in the bunch. Strange for a hospital…" replied Travers.

"For fuck's sake, stop being such an idiot," said Jones. "I mean about Davis and the interrogation!"

"Oh, that, yes, he wanted his stuff back," said Travers. "He wouldn't take extra money for it, just wanted everything back. Makes you wonder how much it was all worth then."

"We'll tell Henry on Monday," said Jones.

Chapter 9

Henry had the feeling that Jeremy had been avoiding him all week. He hadn't been by at all. Henry realized he had missed the boy, especially with the week he had. Jeremy always provided a distraction. To top it all off, it had rained all week, so even Ellie wasn't by with her bell-ringing tricycle. On Saturday he opened the garage and looked at the blueprints for the boat. He called Jeremy over when he saw him walk by.

"Haven't seen you all week," said Henry. "Anything the matter?"

"No, no, just busy with school and friends," said Jeremy.

"Ok, I don't treat you like a kid, so don't treat me like an idiot. Deal?" asked Henry.

"I'm sorry," said Jeremy looking sheepish. "I saw the newspaper on Monday and it said things about you and that lady who was murdered, and I didn't like it."

"I didn't like it either," reflected Henry. "It wasn't all exact, what they wrote. I knew her but I didn't have anything to do with what happened."

"But you did sleep with her, she was your girlfriend?" asked Jeremy.

"Yes, I did see her casually, but no she wasn't my girlfriend. I only saw her a few times, after my wife left me. I didn't cheat. But because I knew her, I can't work on her case anymore, just to keep things separate."

"Are you sad, she's dead?" asked Jeremy.

"Of course, I am, and you can believe me, I had no reason to hurt her, I liked her," said Henry. "Can you help me with the boat? I need to bend these pieces and so far, I'm snapping everything in half," and he showed him two pieces as proof.

"I have to meet a couple of friends, but I can come back and maybe we can figure it out," said Jeremy.

"Great, I'll be here," smiled Henry.

Jeremy came back later in the day and they went over the blueprints and instructions but gave up on that and just added some shelving to store the wood pieces. Little Ellie had wandered over on her tricycle and was playing with Oscar and KC. She came into the garage screaming that KC was going to die and grabbed Henry's hand to drag him over to where the cat was sitting. He felt funny holding her little hand and he smiled.

"See Henry, he's dying, he's sick," cried Ellie as she pointed to KC the tuxedo cat, coughing and hacking.

"He will be fine, no need to worry, cats do that all the time. They eat grass and bugs and they throw up, they don't die," explained Henry as KC jumped on the stairs of the deck. "You can go over and pet him some more."

"Yuck!" said Ellie, running away.

The kids went home for dinner taking with them a few items from Henry's barbecue. As the sun went down Henry sat down with a beer, reclining in his patio chair and stretching his legs. Lisa appeared at the edge of the stairs with a stack of plates and containers.

"I have your dishes here, all cleaned and dried," said Lisa. "You know you don't have to feed my kids all the time but thank you."

"You want a beer?" asked Henry. He offered her a cold one from the cooler next to him. "Saves me having to store leftovers, and feeding a tiny thing like Ellie won't send me to the poor house."

"She's getting spoiled, she won't eat anything from me unless I wrap it up in a foil packet now!" she laughed as she popped the tab of the can and sat down."

"Do you want a glass? I know sometimes ladies prefer not to drink out of the can."

"I'm not that sort of lady, then. Can is fine."

"You're not working tonight?" asked Henry.

"No, I'm off for a few days."

"It must be hard for you, the evenings and nights with the kids."

"It's probably the best for them since I have to work," said Lisa. "On nights, Jeremy is home and they are sleeping anyway, so I'm there in the morning to see them off to school and kindergarten. If I get three twelve hours shifts, I'm free most of the week. It's a bit hard physically, but it saves on daycare also."

"I like your children, they're lots of fun," added Henry.

"Oh, they certainly took a shine to you, but if you get tired of them send them home anytime. I know you don't have kids of your own," said Lisa.

"It's not because I don't like kids," rebuked Henry.

"I'm sorry, I didn't mean anything," apologized Lisa.

"I know," said Henry. "I wanted children, but it never happened. I did speak with Jeremy about the article in the papers, we're all good now."

"Good, so you were seeing that lady that was killed?" asked Lisa.

"Yes, casually, but only after my wife went away," said Henry. "Do you disapprove?"

Lisa laughed, "Not me, the single parent with two kids from different fathers! Everything that's been said about me, I wouldn't throw stones. I would have done the same thing."

"I gather you're not dating anyone?" asked Henry. He relaxed into the conversation but this was different for him. Not interviewing a suspect, but just chatting with a woman about dating!

"No, it's too complicated. That's the standard answer," said Lisa. "I could ramble on about bringing baggage, two kids, shift work, etc. but I think I'm scared stiff of starting again. I wasn't the best judge of character, obviously, and the kids and

I have our routine now. How can I bring someone else into that, without a risk?"

"Plus, I'd have to get dressed up, worry about my weight, and smile sexily while I entertain with small talk!" laughed Lisa.

"Funny, that's exactly the problem I have," concluded Henry.

"Thanks for the beer, Henry. I have to go back for Ellie's bath time."

Henry went down to his basement and laid out the military photos from his box from *Treasures to Share*. He spent the rest of the evening trying to identify the country and the regiment.

On Sunday night, Jeremy came by again and Henry showed him the work he had done so far.

"Wow, those are great," said Jeremy. "Do you have both World War 1 and 2? They don't look Canadian."

"That's the thing, from what I can see they're all Scottish!" acknowledged Henry. He pulled a few of them and explained. "See this one, the two men with moustaches, holding a stick under their arm? They are Royal Scots Pipers."

"What about this one with a skirt?" asked Jeremy.

"That's a kilt, and he's Argyll and Sutherland Highlanders Regiment, World War 1. And those two also in kilts are Seaforth Highlanders."

"And this one, he looks so young, and all the photos are in good condition," said Jeremy.

"He's Royal Scot, he looks just a bit older than you, maybe he was a cadet, or sometimes they lied about their age to enlist," said Henry.

They heard a noise from upstairs and it was Lisa calling for Jeremy.

"We're down in the basement, come in," yelled Henry.

"What are you two up to? What's all this?" she asked. Jeremy explained quickly and quite enthusiastically the work they had been doing. Henry was surprised when she showed interest in the photos, he was used to having his hobby dismissed as foolish by most.

"What are you going to do with them Henry?" she asked.

"I don't know, we can't identify the individuals in the photos, can't tell if they died in the war or have any family left," he said.

"What about a military museum? Would they be interested in getting them?" Lisa said.

"Maybe, that's a great idea, the best so far," said Henry. "I could see if I can find a region at least, I have addresses from some of the old photos in the box. Thanks, I'll investigate it."

"Ok, mister the historian, it's time for some homework," she said to Jeremy as they left.

Notwithstanding the overall very pleasant weekend, Henry felt burdened by the case, the weeks were now going by with no resolution. He hoped that Jones might have had some luck with Russell Davis. He planned to interview Evelyn Blake

McNeill. He wondered whether she was the one who had signed the letter he found in the gun case.

Chapter 10

In a devil-may-care frame of mind, Henry wore both new pants and a new shirt for this Monday at the station. Not trusting the office coffee anymore, at least until Travers dumps this new girlfriend, he stopped at the coffee shop and got a large black to go.

Jones filled him in on the visit with Russell Davis. Travers was looking at a print match for anything at the murder scene against Davis' prints on file. Jones also detailed their interview with Alex's friends Jerry Murphy and Mike Smith.

"The story is pretty much what McNeill said except for where the gun ended up," said Jones. McNeill told us Murphy had it last and threw it away where the car ended up. But Murphy claims he just gave the gun back to McNeill."

"Interesting twist to the story," said Henry. "I had a feeling McNeill was lying. I'm not sure why though."

He pulled the file on the domestic disturbance at the McNeill house from six years ago. The report was brief and nothing had come of it. A neighbour had reported fighting and screaming at the residence.

It looked like a woman had been hit and there was a teenage boy at the home. Evelyn McNeill looked shaken when the constable went to the house. The husband Hugh McNeill was menacing and the teenager was protecting his mother. Evelyn McNeill had refused to lay any charges, saying it was all a misunderstanding, No one was hurt, nothing to see here.

Henry decided to wander over and see if Mrs Evelyn McNeill was at home. The husband and son would be out of the house, it might be a chance for a heart-to-heart. This might have nothing to do with Mary Blake's case. But since Henry was in a time-out for being a bad boy, this was the best use of his time at this moment.

The house was in a new development, just north of town. Typical of a real estate agent, Henry considered, they were always the first ones on deals. Mrs McNeill was at home, and surprised to see DS Stafford. She remembered him from the funeral. Right away Henry could tell she was a Blake sister. She was a younger version of Joan and Mary. She looked to be in her mid-forties, tall and slim with blonde hair. She was wearing trendy pants, a tight top and a scarf knotted around her neck. Her demeanour was tense and anxious. She reminded Henry of a scared cat likely to pounce at the slightest noise.

"Would you like something to drink, tea or coffee?" Evelyn asked.

"Just water perhaps," said Henry.

"Are you here to tell me about new developments, did you find Mary's killer yet?" she asked.

"I'm afraid not, I'm sorry, we are still investigating, we have a few leads," said Henry who found it easier to lie on duty. He also withheld any of his dealings with young Alex at this time, unless she brought it up, of course. Somehow, he suspected Alex hadn't shared that part of his life with his mother.

"It's about something else, Mrs McNeill. You are aware that a gun belonging to your sister Mary was stolen before the incident."

"Yes, but I thought it didn't have anything to do with the murder. She wasn't shot."

"No, she wasn't, but you see we can't have a weapon running loose around town, I'm sure you understand. Do you know how Mary came into possession of the firearm?"

She took a sip of her coffee, looking pensively into thin air. Where did she go to, wondered Henry.

"Mrs McNeill?"

"No, I don't know, she just mentioned having it, a long time ago."

Henry pulled out a piece of paper from his jacket pocket, unfolded it and read, "Keep this in case you need it. If I hold on to it, I might use it. Signed E."

"Oh, I forgot about that," sighed Evelyn. "Yes, I remember now, I did give it to her, or rather she got the gun for me and I handed it back."

"Care to explain this a bit further?" asked Henry.

"There was a rash of break-ins, years ago, and I asked Mary to get me a gun, just for safety's sake, you know. Then I feared it and gave it back to her, for safekeeping."

"The letter implies she might need a gun, and that should you keep it you might use it. What did you mean by that?"

"Oh, that was just a joke, between us, I would never shoot anyone!" replied Evelyn.

"And do you have any idea where the gun might be now Mrs McNeill?"

"No, I haven't seen it in years, I'm sorry Detective, I can't help you. I have a doctor's appointment in a half hour and I must go. It was nice to meet you."

Henry was ushered out the door, like a smelly dog. In the time he had known Mary, he had coined her as an interesting character, that's before he met the sisters!

Since he was out on the road, he might as well push to Chesterville and see what he could get out of Joan. Seeing the letter might incite a few confidences.

The familiar bell rang as Henry came into the shop. Not much had changed in the front end, but a few of the larger pieces had gone, making room for more display of the smaller items. Henry could hear voices in the back, Joan for one and the other was a man. The discussion seemed confrontational. Joan came to the front followed by a tall man, with dark hair and a moustache. Henry had seen that face before, many times. Posted on for-sale signs across the neighbourhood and six feet tall on a billboard out of town. He was real estate agent Hugh McNeill. He brushed past Henry, not bothering to introduce himself. McNeill glanced back at Joan and said, "This isn't over." Joan turned towards Henry and smiled a most wicked smile.

"Oh, hello Inspector Stafford," said Joan, who could never quite get his rank right. "Any news for me on catching the guilty party?"

"I'm afraid not, not yet anyway," said Henry. "I'm sorry but I couldn't help but overhear, do you have a problem with your brother-in-law?

"Nothing that I can't manage," sighed Joan. "Been dealing with him for years. It's just that now Mary is gone, he wants me to sell the shop and the property."

"Is there any particular reason for that?" asked Henry. "Mary had a will I imagine."

"Yes, she did, and based on it, everything is split two ways between us sisters. Hugh wants to get his hands on Evelyn's share. But I'm not ready to sell. No need for you to worry, it's a private family discussion. How can I help you?"

"I'm here to talk about the stolen gun."

"Ah, yes, that. But I told you I didn't know anything about it," insisted Joan.

"I know, but I found a letter, in the gun case, which might stir your memory," said Henry. He pulled out the paper and opened it. "Does the writing or even the signature bring anything to mind? To be honest with you I already spoke with your sister Evelyn and I do have part of the story."

"Well then, that's it, you know," said Joan. "Mary obtained the gun for Evelyn, but she didn't want it and gave it back. End of story, don't know where it ended up."

"Why did Evelyn need a gun in the first place?" asked Henry. "And don't tell me a wave of break-ins, she lives in Winchester, as do I…I can't recall any such wave and I'm with the police…"

"It all comes out in the end, doesn't it," said Joan. "All right, as sisters we look after each other, Mary was the strongest of us. She didn't stand for any bullying, but Evelyn did."

"There were things between Hugh and Evelyn?" asked Henry. "I did see a police report for a disturbance, a while back."

"Yes, but Evelyn is weak, she likes her place in society, a father for her son, and all that bullshit. Mary was worried about her and got her the gun. You know the rest from the letter."

"Has Hugh ever been violent with Evelyn or Alexander?" worried Henry.

"Not that I know of, but I wouldn't be surprised if he ever did," confessed Joan. "You see it's more perverse than that, Hugh is very controlling. It's in the small things, day to day. Like when Evelyn found herself a job as a receptionist for an insurance broker. Hugh didn't like that so he cut up all her work clothes. He repeatedly found ways to make her late for work. Finally, she quit and stayed home."

"Do you think he knows about the gun?" asked Henry. "Was he angry at Mary for standing up to him?"

"I don't know, there was no love lost between the two of them, that's for sure. And there is something else too..."

"What?" asked Henry.

"In the early years, when Hugh first came to the family, he made advances to Mary," said Joan. "Of course, she turned him away in no uncertain terms. But that didn't help matters."

"Thank you for your confidence, Joan, you have my number if there is anything please contact me," said Henry. He left the store with more questions and he knew he needed to put it all together, look at the bigger picture.

He drove back to the station, and all hell was breaking loose when he got to his desk.

"We've got him!" said Jones as he grabbed his jacket. "There was a match for prints on Russell Davis. From the glass display case. And guess what?"

"What?" asked Henry, hoping for a break in the case, finally.

"We did a search of his place, found the two invoice pads..." smiled Jones. "We're bringing him in! Constables and a marked car with a cherry on top."

Chapter 11

Russell Davis was brought into the interview room. As usual DI Rowley, as lead investigator, had been given a summary of the events leading to this arrest.

"Would you like to conduct the interview, Sir?" asked Jones.

"Good, it's all good, perfect," said Rowley. "No, it's your show now Jones, so go ahead."

Jones and Travers did the honours and went in to start the questioning. Henry was behind the glass, just observing, and that was killing him.

"Hello, Mister Davis, nice of you to come in and answer our questions," said Jones. He introduced himself and Travers formally for the record.

"As you know we found your prints on the glass display case, in the shop *Treasures to Share*, where Miss Mary Blake was assaulted and later died of injuries. Care to tell us more about this?"

"I have nothing to do with the Mrs dying," said Davis.

"We also found two invoice pads, which had gone missing, taken from the top of that same display case. Found them in your apartment, care to go over it all again?"

"Ok, I did go to the shop, on Monday morning, after work, I drove up," said Davis.

"At what time?" asked Travers, as he clicked his pen ready to take notes.

"Around 10 am, I wanted my stuff back, so I thought I'd talk to her again, about getting the names of the people who bought it, so I could get it back," explained Davis.

"You went in, confronted her, she said no and you pushed her, and she fell, bumping her head on the corner," said Jones.

"No, I did go in but I heard voices in the back, her and a man arguing," pleaded Davis.

"Arguing about what?" asked Jones.

"I couldn't hear all of it. The man said, 'You're screwing everyone else, so why not me?' I saw the invoice pads. I figured I could just get the names of the people who bought my stuff that way. I grabbed them and ran out."

"That's convenient, for an excuse. What do you think Travers?"

"Yep, but it's your word against the evidence, isn't it?' said Travers. "I'm comfortable with the evidence."

"Travers let's book him," said Jones as he left the room. Travers proceeded with the charges and told Davis that a lawyer would be assigned to him unless he had one in mind already.

Behind the glass Henry was pensive. The evidence was strong, you can't deny that. But Henry had laughed at Travers when he had suggested it might have been two thefts, one after the other. But what if he had been right, not two thefts, but two different people, one after the other? One was a thief, the other a murderer. A gut feeling didn't convict people, evidence did, that, Henry knew.

Grilling had lost some of its magic for Henry, so he picked up a large all-dressed pizza from Mary's Restaurant. He went straight to his basement; he was planning to follow Lisa's suggestions and investigate museums that would accept the military photos.

The few items in the box that showed an address, led to West Lothian, more precisely Uphall Station. Henry got the atlas out and saw it was west of Edinburgh. He could mention the photos at the Legion. Some of the old folks there might have an idea about museums, so Henry made some notes. There were also other photos, World War 2 and some showing India, and group photos of soldiers in training. He was enjoying these discoveries.

Jeremy wandered over, just in time to grab the last slice of pizza. He wanted to look at the photos again. From the pile in the box, he pulled one of a young lady, hand-written on the back "Anne, 16 years old". He showed it to Henry and said, "She's pretty."

"That she is," said Henry, and he showed Jeremy a few more of the girl with others who looked like sisters.

"So, you know a lot about women then?" asked Jeremy.

Henry laughed, "Not at all, why do you ask? Are there girls at school you are starting to notice?"

"Maybe," said Jeremy.

"You know about not getting a girl in trouble?" wondered Henry. He wasn't in the mood for a bird and the bees conversation.

"Get real, my mother is a nurse, my sister has dolls with all the right parts," laughed Jeremy. "No, it's not about that, but how do you know how to pick the right one?"

"I'm the worst man to ask that question, I never picked anyone," said Henry.

"So how did you end up with a wife and a girlfriend then?" Jeremy was curious.

"They chose me, probably because I was the path of least resistance," said Henry.

"What does that mean?"

"That they could boss me around and I wouldn't make a fuss about it," said Henry.

"Do I just wait until a girl picks me?"

"That didn't work out too well for me, so no. I'd say you need to take a more active part in your life. That's what went wrong with me, I just let things happen."

"Well, how do I know which one to pick?" insisted Jeremy.

"It's like a long trip, you know if they say you're going on a school trip, on the bus for like four hours, who do you want to sit with? Somebody cute or somebody fun?

"I see, I need to pick a girl that's cute and fun!" said Jeremy.

"Way to go! Now, once you figure out how to do that, you come back and tell me!" smirked Henry.

"Do you know we might have to move?" said Jeremy.

"No, why?" A scary feeling came over him. The family next door was now part of his routine, and he didn't like change. He liked certainty and patterns. That Jeremy would come over, that Ellie would ring her bell and run her tricycle up his driveway. He couldn't see the faces of new neighbours; he liked things the way they were.

"Yes, the landlord is putting the house for sale, so Mom says we may have to move. The new owners might want the house for themselves," explained Jeremy. "But we would move in town, so I could still come over."

"I guess we have to wait and see," said Henry.

Sunday morning Henry mowed the front lawn and felt sick to his stomach when he saw the for-sale sign in Lisa's front yard. The disgust was compounded by seeing the face of Hugh McNeill grinning back at him! For the rest of the day, Henry locked himself in his garage. He pounded on nails with such energy, they all went in with one strike of the hammer.

For Lisa, the sale of the house was a sad prospect. She was originally from Ottawa and had done her nurse's training there. She had taken a job at the Cornwall Community Hospital shortly after graduation. Jeremy's father was in Ottawa but had never shown interest in his son. Ellie's father, Peter, she met at the Cornwall Hospital; he was a fellow nurse.

It had all gone well at the start but when Ellie came along, Peter began to resent Jeremy's presence and that created tension. It wasn't a matter for Lisa to choose between Peter and Jeremy. They went their separate ways, but Peter wanted to be in Ellie's life. Working with Peter became a nightmare and when the opening at the Winchester Hospital came up last year, she jumped on it. Winchester was close enough for Peter to see Ellie, with just enough distance between him and Lisa. Jeremy could also stay connected with his Cornwall friends. They made the move and settled in well. But if the house sold, they would have to move again and small rental houses were rare. This place had a reasonable rent, three bedrooms and as it turned out a lovely neighbour. It was within walking distance from the hospital and the school. She doubted she could find anything to match within her price range.

Chapter 12

To build a conviction for Russell Davis, they needed to ask more questions and understand his motive. Cleared of all suspicions, Henry was back as lead investigator. He had been told as soon as he showed up on Monday. Unofficially of course, as DI Dick Rowley was still in charge of the investigation on paper. But he was often missing in action and strangely non-committal. Henry was starting to enjoy Mondays again, especially now that Travers had a new girlfriend. That one worked at the local bakery and supplied her new lover with samples. Henry hoped this was going to be a long-lasting relationship.

Russell Davis entered the interview room, looking like a mess, tired and depressed. Henry put a styrofoam cup with black coffee in front of him. Davis took it eagerly. His appointed lawyer was present and eager to get started.

"I didn't do it," he said. "I didn't push her, argue with her, or even see her when I went in. This is all wrong."

"You said you wanted to get back items you sold her?" asked Henry. "What were the pieces in question?"

"I sold her things from my grandmother's house. She died and we had to clear her rental unit," explained Davis. "But I told the shopkeeper that the boxes came from a moving van, stuff left behind."

"Can you give us a list of items? Now that we have recovered the sales invoices, we can confirm what you are saying," said Henry. "What did you want so badly, that you would kill for?"

"I DIDN'T KILL HER," yelled Davis. "I didn't care about the jewellery, the books, or the figurines - all junk to me. But there was a box of photos, some military photos from World War 1 and 2."

Henry realized they might be talking about HIS box of photos. It was uncanny, it led right back to him.

"What about the photos, what made you think they were worth more than what Mary Blake gave you for them?" asked Henry.

"It's something my mother told me recently. That Grandpa had photos from Scotland and England. Some were family but the military ones were from a collection," he explained. "Worth a lot of money, it was said, especially those showing British military in India."

"And why were they valuable?" asked Henry.

"Because it is said that some show a member of the Royal Family! That's why," said Davis.

Henry concluded the interview, made notes and went directly to Staff Sergeant Glenn's office. Henry went over Russell Davis' statement and told Glenn that he had the box of photos at the centre of this investigation.

"Should we let DI Rowley know, Sir?" asked Stafford.

"I will tell him," said Glenn. "Right now, he's gone to the Legion. He knows somebody there. Anyway, back to our business. The box should be considered evidence."

Henry knew it had to be returned. Mentally cursing the fact that he was the focus of attention again, Henry went home to get the items. He sadly packed everything up carefully and grabbed the bill of sale. He intended to make a copy showing that the purchase was in good order. Fortunately, the receipt showed no mention of a discount, it had stayed between him and Mary.

Henry was ill at ease again; he didn't want any of this. He wanted to go back to slow days, a good cup of coffee and the occasional doughnut. Mind you, after his dating conversation with Lisa, he now opted for old-fashioned plain rather than filled or dipped. It was a sad reckoning but with his birthday coming up, he needed to put a bit of effort in.

Home was quiet now; Henry had even lost interest in grilling. When Jeremy came over one evening to work on the photos, he found Henry sitting on his deck, pensive and lethargic. Henry explained that the photos were gone, part of the murder case. Jeremy had lots of questions about it.

"What are the odds, thinking about all the stuff that goes in and out of that antique shop, that you're the one with the prize!" said Jeremy. "Will they give them back to you when they're done?"

"Possibly," said Henry. "I have a bill of sale, and Mary had paperwork from when she bought the box from Davis."

"And do you believe what that guy said about the photos being worth a lot of money?"

"I don't know, I wasn't looking for that. To be honest with you, I don't know what a member of the Royal Family would look like, aside from the Queen of course."

"I guess we will have to wait and see," added Jeremy. "But there are other things we can do in the meantime. How about your computer? Do you want to do something with it?"

"Like what? If I don't catalogue my photos, what do I need it for?" asked Henry.

"My friend showed me some games and loaned me a few. I can go home and see what I have. You might like some of them," suggested Jeremy.

Henry didn't want to do anything, but he could see Jeremy was trying and he didn't want to disappoint him. "Ok, let's see what you've got."

Jeremy came back with games and an extra joystick. Henry now had his own. They turned everything on and inserted a game cartridge.

"Let's start with something easy, you might like that racing game *Pole Position.* It's like driving a car.

You go first," said Jeremy. In the first round, Henry was oversteering and always on the shoulder rather than the track, sharp turns were his downfall. Then he got better and could hold his own. They moved up to *Pit Stop 2* and raced against each other. They laughed, bounced and moved left to right as if they were really in the car.

"One more," said Jeremy. "Let's play *Bruce Lee*, for that one you kick and fight off the bad guys - good practice for a policeman. The joystick is for moving the character along, up and down ladders, that sort of thing. Then you use the buttons to kick and punch. Got it?

"How complicated can it be, let's go," said Henry with the self-confidence of an adult who never played an action game before. The reality was going to strike him soon!

Jeremy played first to show him how it went and coached him when it was his turn.

"Jump! Jump!" yelled Jeremy. "Hit the button, kick, come on! You suck at this!"

"It's the little music, it's distracting," said Henry. "I just need practice, that's all." Henry secretly decided to buy that game the next time he was out.

"I have to go home now, but that was fun, thanks Henry," said Jeremy, gathering up his cartridges.

"I'll get some games, we can have a showdown on the weekend," said Henry. He had spent a fun evening and almost forgot about the photos.

Chapter 13

The due process of conviction was grinding along, and although Russell Davis was still crying foul, he was awaiting trial. There was no word yet on Henry's photos, they would be in evidence until sentencing he figured. In the meantime, he had looked up the military museum in Scotland, the West Lothian area, and wrote to them explaining what he had. Unfortunately for everyone, Travers had moved on to a new girlfriend. No more samples of fresh baked goods. This time around he was seeing a beautician from Cornwall. Priority bookings for haircuts were a far cry from French Croissant and Chocolatines thought Henry.

Hugh McNeill's mug and moustache still greeted Henry every night when he came down the street. But now, the *For Sale* sign was plastered with a *Sold* sticker. Lisa came over to his car when she noticed him pulling in. Little Ellie ran up to him and said, "We're not moving, Henry!" as she jumped up and down. Lisa laughed and explained.

"The house is sold, but the new owner is keeping it as a rental. Some sort of investment property. We don't have to move, I'm so happy. I like it here; the kids are settled."

"That's great news, I'm happy for you," said Henry. He was well pleased with the news himself. "Do you know who bought it?"

"No, it was all done through the real estate agent and the lawyer," said Lisa. "I don't care, as long as we don't have to move. There doesn't seem to be a rent increase either. We're celebrating with a movie night; do you want to come over later?" she asked. "I can send Jeremy with the membership card and you guys could go and pick up the VCR and movie rentals. If you don't mind, of course."

"Get Care Bears, Care Bears," said Ellie.

Jeremy came and asked Henry if he had rented movies or video discs before and had his membership card. This was going to be yet another new experience for him. They headed over to *Winchester TV & Video Shack*.

"Mom must be really happy about this, normally she never lets us do anything like this on a weekday," said Jeremy. "It's good though because the Shack has deals for weekdays. What sort of movies do you like?"

"I don't know, I guess we'll have to see the selection," said Henry. And he wasn't disappointed, it was wall-to-wall movies.

Jeremy grabbed a Care Bears movie for Ellie. "It doesn't matter which one it is, she'll watch it ten times over before we have to return it." He pointed to a few others for themselves.

"How about *48 Hrs*, it's a cop movie?" proposed Jeremy. Henry shook his head; he's had enough of policing for now. Jeremy showed him another box and that got vetoed. It was a beach and lifeguard tape. "I'm not watching two hours of girls in bathing suits, yelling "He's drowning, he's drowning!" said Henry. "What does your mother like? Love stories?"

"Nah, she's over that," laughed Jeremy. "How about we get both *Flashdance* and *Raiders of the Lost Ark*? One for us and one for her, although I have a feeling, she'll go for the Harrison Ford one."

"Sounds good, let's go," said Henry. They got the tapes and a storage case with the VCR and wiring. The rentals were good for three days.

This was the first time Henry went over to the house next door since Edgar had left with his wife. Lisa had made it a pleasant space, with kids' stuff everywhere, and the house had life in it. Jeremy set up the VCR and loaded Ellie's movie first. They could expect her to fall asleep quickly once it began. Henry and Jeremy laid out the other two movies on the kitchen table and asked Lisa to pick one. They both had their fingers crossed for the Harrison Ford movie. There was a big sigh of relief when she chose it. She was no fool but it had been nice of them to at least try…

Ellie jumped on the sofa, right beside Henry with her blue Care Bear, Jeremy was on the other side, and Lisa brought in snacks and took the big chair. As expected, Ellie fell asleep twenty minutes into the movie. Lisa put her to bed and *Raiders* started. Henry looked around and felt good, this was nice. A few minutes in, his pager vibrated and the light of the display glowed. It was a 999. Not good news.

"Can I use your phone?" asked Henry. Lisa nodded and he made the call to dispatch.

"I'm sorry, I have to go, an emergency," said Henry.

They looked at him with worry in their eyes. "Be careful," said Lisa. And right then, while *Indiana Jones* cracked a whip on the bad guys, Henry Stafford realized he mattered. And that was all he'd ever wanted. He'd just never put a name to it before.

The emergency call had been for a fire, at the back of *Treasures to Share*, the antique shop of Joan Blake. It had come in at 9 p.m. They had called Henry because of the past events, and this was suspicious. There was more to it, he knew, but the dispatcher hadn't gone into details.

When Henry arrived at the shop, off King Street, fire services and an ambulance were on site. It was part of the standard call. The constable had delimited the perimeter. It was at the back, beside the door. On the ground was a sheet covering what seemed to be a body.

Henry approached the lead fireman. "What have we got here?" asked Henry.

"The coroner is on its way, we have a burnt body," said the Captain. He took Henry over and peeled back the sheet. Henry glanced and felt sick to his stomach, the smell was beyond anything he had ever encountered before. There laid a figure, blackened and unrecognizable. "Dear God," thought Henry. "What a way to go."

"Luckily, the whole building didn't catch fire, could've been the whole block," said the Captain. "By the looks of it, see the melted jerry can. The victim had fuel with him."

"Might have been planning to burn down the shop?" asked Henry.

"Very well could be," said the fireman. "The thing is he didn't have time, something set off the gasoline and he caught on fire before anything else."

"Rough way to go," said Henry.

The coroner was now beside the body and getting ready to move it out. Photos were taken, and the guys were gathering what evidence they could. There did not seem to be any witnesses. It was par for the course at this time of day downtown.

"Don't ask," said Dr Carlisle, the coroner. "I won't be able to tell you what set this off until I do the autopsy, sorry Henry."

"Identification?" asked Henry, but he knew the answer. He would have to wait.

The crowd of onlookers was now growing, drawn in by the sirens and flashing lights. Joan Blake and Evelyn McNeill were gathered by the police tape but held back by a constable. Henry went over to talk to them. Joan was shaking and crying. Disbelief was all over her face. Evelyn was her nervous self.

"Joan, I expect you weren't in the shop when this started?" asked Henry. He nodded to Mrs McNeill; the usual good evening greeting would have seemed out of place.

"No, I was home," said Joan. "But when I heard the commotion, I knew it was the shop and Evelyn was with me visiting. This is terrible, I don't know how I can come back to this place again."

"How can anyone do this?" asked Evelyn. "It's beyond belief."

Henry recommended they all went home and he would follow up with them tomorrow. For now, the shop was safe and they wouldn't know any more about the victim until the coroner did his work. Constables would be on site for a while, so best for the family to go home. They reluctantly left.

Henry stayed behind for a while, talking with the firefighters and emergency technicians who had been first to arrive. They had not seen anyone around or running away from the scene. For most of them, the recent events had been well beyond their routine in this small town. There was certainly a common thread of disasters for this shop and family. There would be another list to build, Russell Davis was not a suspect in this, he was behind bars. Someone had attempted to burn down the shop, and it was targeted, but why? Henry wondered about the burned victim. Was someone trying to stop him or was it something more personal?

Chapter 14

Henry opened one eye and saw the red numbers on the clock glowing at 7:45 am. He had overslept, but it had been a short night. Sitting inches from his face was KC, the black and white cat, voicing his disappointment in sharp and cursory sounds. Cats were creatures of routine, and so was Henry, an idyllic match if each side held to its end of the bargain. This morning Henry had not, KC informed him.

Oscar, the tabby, was laying on Henry's head, not saying a word but tacitly agreeing with the disapproval put forth by KC. There were a few kibbles left in the feed bowl but KC preferred fresh and full. Henry, new to the world of cat ownership, had discovered late that for domestic felines, there were masters and waiters. Cats were the former, humans the latter. A fact confirmed when Henry went to the washroom, followed by KC who sat at the edge of the bathtub voicing yet, another comment. Henry sighed and turned on the tap, the cat wanted to drink from the running bathtub faucet. Henry had done this once, thinking it was cute. Little did he know! Even Paula had never been this demanding. But at ldoubleast they were affectionate.

They purred when Henry touched them, a rare occurrence with Paula.

Henry recalled last night's events and the order of the day would be to find out what happened at the antique shop in Chesterville, again. There was a curse on the place, and to complicate matters they now had multiple crimes, motives and perpetrators. Overwhelmed, Henry considered packing a suitcase and running away from home. He quickly dismissed the thought; the cats depended on him.

Even though he woke up later than usual, he would not be late for work. He lived on Clarence Street, the police station was one block away, across the street from that was a school, and next was the hospital. The benefits of working and living in a small town.

Stopping first to grab a coffee, Jones and Travers already knew what happened. DI Rowley was at his desk, realizing he now had another homicide to deal with.

"Got yourself a BBQ, last night boss? Didn't invite us?" said Travers to Henry.

"Have more respect, Travers, will you, someone died," remarked Henry.

"Sorry," said Travers.

Clearing his desk, Henry started the report including what the emergency services had noticed. He made a few calls and planned to visit the coroner once the autopsy was done. Henry didn't like to attend autopsies. In this case, he wouldn't be able to stomach it. It was never a good thing to be seen as uncomfortable at these proceedings; the guys could tease you for months.

Joan Blake called him, just after ten. She was a nervous wreck and Henry couldn't blame her.

"Evelyn just called me, she doesn't know where Hugh or Alex are," said Joan. "I told her to go and see you, perhaps she needs to put in a missing person's report or something."

"That was good advice," said Henry. "What about Alex and Hugh, do they often stay out all night?" Henry considered whether Hugh was having an affair and if Alex had just crashed at a friend's place.

"With the body last night, Evelyn was concerned, could it be Hugh or Alex?" asked Joan.

"We don't know anything at this point. It could be two unrelated events, so it's best if she does put in a missing person's report," said Henry. "Normally we ask for a 24-hour wait period but given everything that's happened, it's wise. I will wait for her then."

"Thank you," said Joan.

Henry called Jones over and he told him about Alex and Hugh McNeill and Evelyn coming in to report missing persons. He wondered when they were seen last.

"I just had a call from the front, Jerry Murphy and his father are here," said Jones. "They want to press charges against Hugh McNeill for assault on the son Jerry."

"Take a number!" said Henry. "God, get me off this merry-go-round. You take the Murphy complaint since you already talked to Jerry and I'll wait for Evelyn.

"We should sell tickets for this murder case. We could make a bit for our Christmas Party," said Travers.

Jones took Jerry Murphy and his father to the interview room in the front. He had his notepad with him and was already clicking his ballpoint pen. Seemingly warming it up for a marathon.

Jerry Murphy had a bruised cheek, a black eye and a cut lip. The eighteen-year-old was in bad shape. Jones recognized Jerry's father, Len Murphy, a city employee with municipal works. He was a sturdy fellow, a bit on the heavy side, the opposite of his son who was tall and skinny.

"Care to tell me what happened?" asked Jones.

"I was attacked by Hugh McNeill," said young Jerry.

"And when was that?" continued Jones.

"It was yesterday, around supper time, maybe 6 o'clock. I was coming home from work and he was waiting for me just before my house," explained Jerry.

"I know my son has been in some trouble lately, but it's nobody's business but our own, how we discipline him," said Len Murphy.

"William Campbell didn't want to press charges for the stolen car, from what I heard," said Jones.

"No, I talked to him," said Jerry's father. "I offered some compensation. It wouldn't help the kids to get a criminal record."

"Jerry, do you know why Hugh McNeill hit you?" asked Jones.

"Yes, I've been hanging out with his son, as you know. And he blamed me for leading Alex into trouble, with the joyriding, stealing the car, and all that mess," said Jerry. "But that's not really how it went, Alex was just as much a leader as me or Mike Smith."

"And did you tell him that?" asked Jones.

"I tried but I didn't have much time to explain," said Jerry. "He punched me, and I fell and he kept hitting me until a neighbour called him out."

"I want charges brought to him, he has no right to just attack my son, just like that," said Mr Murphy. "I think the boy has learned his lesson and won't be hanging about with those two anymore. I think he deserves a chance more than a beating."

"Yes, I see your point," said Jones. "We will do a police report and lay charges. I'll just need all the specifics and you may be called again to testify."

"Sure, whatever it takes," said Jerry.

"Did you get checked out by a doctor?" asked Jones. "You might want to do that and take the report back to us."

"Thank you, Sergeant," said Len and Jerry nodded.

By the time Jones got back to his desk, the clerk had rung Henry to say that Mrs Evelyn McNeill was at the reception. Henry had heard rumours that the admin clerk was going to ask for a raise due to the extra work she had been given since the murder, filing was piling up.

Evelyn McNeill was tense as a guitar string. She looked thinner and more nervous than Henry had ever seen her before. He offered her a seat and had a pen and paper ready.

"Thank you for coming in, Mrs McNeill," said Henry. "I'm sorry about all this, it must be hard on you and your family. Can you tell me when you last saw both Alex and your husband?"

"You can call me Evelyn if you wish. Alex, I saw him yesterday evening," said Evelyn. "He was mostly trying to stay out of his father's way. You see Hugh had found out about some trouble Alex had been in."

"And did he say where he was going?" asked Henry.

"He said he'd go stay with friends for a while," explained Evelyn. "But since then, he didn't call and the friends I asked haven't seen him."

"And what about your husband, when did you see him last?" asked Henry. He could feel the tension in her answers.

"Around 7 pm, and Alex I saw a bit later," said Evelyn. "But when I came back from Chesterville and tried to reach both, I couldn't find them. I had a dreadful feeling one of them might be that burnt body."

"Does your husband ever stay away, for an extended period?" asked Henry.

"You mean like having an affair?" asked Evelyn. "I've no doubt he is unfaithful but more local, short-term flings, no overnight stuff."

"Given everything that has happened lately, are you aware of anything suspicious going on? Is anyone wanting to hurt him? Any financial issues?"

Tears ran down her cheeks and Henry handed her the box of tissues. He gave her a minute to compose herself and she went on.

"It's all a mess, my family just blew apart," said Evelyn. "There's always been tension between Hugh and Mary. She turned him down so many times. And I knew. Things with Alex were difficult, Hugh's way of keeping him in line, and his discipline did not work well. If anything, it made him rebel more. Alex graduated high school but couldn't decide on work or college. He was in and out of work often. Couldn't seem to find a direction."

"And for Hugh, financially?" asked Henry, feeling that financial pressures might have played a role in Hugh trying to get Joan to sell the shop and building.

"You name it, we had it…" sighed Evelyn. "There was some abuse, and all the times I tried to cover it up and pretend we were the perfect family…it just blew up in my face. He lost a lot of business lately, you know real-estate, it's all about who you know and your reputation."

"Was your husband in trouble, with anyone in particular?" Henry persisted.

"He had a big contract to sell a new development. It was slow, so he made promises that the contractor could not fulfil, so they got into a fight. Then people didn't trust Hugh anymore, so he got fewer referrals. The contractor was Charles Brown, and there's bad blood between them."

"I've taken all this down and will put the information out that we are looking for both Alex and Hugh," said Henry. "I will need information on the cars they drive. I will get in touch if we hear anything, along the same line please call me if one or the other returns home."

"Thank you, Officer," said Evelyn. "I can't get it out of my mind, the fire yesterday. I'm so scared it could be one of them…Alex."

"We don't know anything yet, so please take care of yourself," said Henry. He showed her out of the station.

Henry felt like he'd been run over by a train. He couldn't think straight, with all this information and faces running through his mind. He was physically tired, and no amount of coffee was going to fix that. Another cup and he would be an over-caffeinated babbling idiot. DI Rowley had been no help at all. He was more like a ghost, just planning his retirement. Henry would have to brainstorm with Jones and Travers. Somewhere over his shoulder, he thought he heard his guardian angel slap his knee and laugh.

Chapter 15

Dr Carlisle notified Henry that the post-mortem was done and that he was ready to share his findings. Carlisle would be at the hospital morgue all day. Henry asked Jones to come along, they could stop by the hospital cafeteria for lunch first and see Dr Carlisle afterwards. Henry opted not to ask the doctor to join them for lunch. He had learned his lesson the one and only time he did ask him along. Dr Carlisle likes to go over his work, any time, any place, and that had put Henry off his lunch.

The coroner, fortunately, cut to the chase and didn't go over all the finer details of the autopsy. But Dr Carlisle was in the mood for a guessing game.

"I did the autopsy and I'll take three guesses on the cause of death?" said Carlisle.

"Immolation, asphyxiation, strangulation," tried Henry.

As if they were on a game show and had submitted a wrong answer Carlisle went, "Wanh-wanh."

"Ok, I give up," said Henry, who wasn't in the mood for this.

"He did burn, but first he was shot…bullet to the heart," said Dr Carlisle. "There was a second bullet that hit the jerrycan full of gas, starting the explosion that set the body on fire."

"Could we not even get one thing right? A simple murder? What's up with these people?" asked Jones.

"How do you know that the first bullet hit his heart, and the second bullet got the gas can?" asked Henry. "Could it not have been the reverse?"

"Simple, if the bullet had hit the gas can first, while he was still alive, he would have let go of it," replied Carlisle. "As it stands his hand was still grasping the handle, or rather melted into it, when we found him."

"Do you have an identity?" asked Henry.

"We had to go to dental records, of course, that's why it took a bit longer," said Dr Carlisle. "It's Hugh McNeill."

"There you go, boss. We've solved one case!" said Jones. "We found the missing person!"

"Idiot," sighed Henry. "Do we have a match on the bullet? A bit of good luck wouldn't go amiss, just about now."

"Not yet, it's gone for testing, but there's a backlog," said Dr Carlisle. "I'll call you as soon as I hear."

"I guess you'll have to see Mrs McNeill again," said Jones.

"Yay! And the winner is…Stafford!"

This time Henry called the Public Health Unit at the hospital and asked if there was someone available to go with him to see Evelyn McNeill. He told them about this situation and the run of hard luck the family had in recent weeks. Aware of the fragile state Evelyn was in, he didn't know what to expect. Support would be appreciated. Henry picked up a nurse on his way to Evelyn's and he filled her in on the specifics. Evelyn had a family but this was affecting everyone and they all would need support, as he saw it. At Mary's funeral, he had learned that Mr Blake was in a retirement home and not well himself.

When Evelyn heard the knock and saw the marked car in the driveway, she knew her life was about to change. Henry first introduced Nurse Pat Leblanc, and they went to the living room.

"You have news?" asked Evelyn. "About Mary or Hugh? Alex? God, the list is getting long." And she collapsed into tears. Nurse Leblanc, pulled in closer and put her arm around her.

"We have an identification for the victim of the fire," he began. "It's your husband." Henry wished with all his heart that he could be somewhere else, but he wasn't and he had to conclude this.

"We also know that he was shot first before the fire started," said Henry. He was hoping this fact would tell Evelyn that her husband had not suffered and was dead before the burn. It's a small consolation, but for some, it matters that their loved one didn't suffer in the end.

"So, we have hope for Alex?" asked Evelyn. She had slumped forward, her head in her hands, in disbelief.

"No news on Alex, we are still trying to locate him," said Henry. The nurse looked at him and with a nod told him she could manage this and that he could go.

"I'm going to leave you with Nurse Leblanc and she can call for a ride once you have someone else with you. "Perhaps you can call Joan or a friend to stay with you?"

"I will be in touch again soon," said Henry as he thanked Patricia for her help.

Henry made his way back home; he didn't stop by the station. At this time of day and with his last duty, no one expected him back. He stopped by the refrigerator, popped open a can of beer and stretched on the couch. He was done.

Chapter 16

The next morning Henry dragged himself into the station and went full deluxe with a double cream and sugar coffee and a glazed doughnut. Jones was in but Travers had called saying he would be late, something with traffic coming up from Cornwall. More likely a late night with the beautician thought Henry, with a touch of envy. DI Rowley was at his desk, flipping through the local paper.

Jones had no news at this end from their search for Alex McNeill or his car. They had alerted the nearby stations in the Counties, the local police in Cornwall and the RCMP. Henry suggested he also contact Jerry and Len Murphy. No charges could be laid now, as the perpetrator was deceased. Henry would talk to Staff Sergeant Glenn, to see if he could put some pressure on forensics for the match of the bullet. This case couldn't drag on any more than it already had. A trial date was coming up for Russell Davis in the manslaughter case of Mary Blake, but Henry was still not convinced he was guilty.

Travers came in and kept a low profile. He didn't say hi to anyone and kept his head bowed while he went to his desk. Henry noticed there was something different about him but couldn't put his finger on it.

Jones came over to his desk and stood in front of Henry with his back to Travers.

"What's up with him?" asked Jones. "Did you notice his haircut? And something is going on with his eyebrows.

Henry looked up and yes, there it was, a new haircut and was it an eyebrow pluck! Oh, my god! Travers kept his hair short, so it would be hard to mess up a haircut, one would think. But they would be wrong. It was still short but it was uneven, he was somehow out of balance, left to right.

"Hey Travers, did you pay for that haircut or did it come complimentary with the eyebrow pluck?" said Henry. It wasn't particularly nice of him to say that, but Travers and Jones had teased him plenty, so now it was payback time.

Jones remembered that Travers's new girlfriend was a beautician, so that explained a lot. Travers tried to make himself disappear behind his monitor.

"Maybe he paid for it in nature, if that's the case it says a lot about his performance," said Jones.

"Yes, certainly not a three-star rating," said Henry with a wide grin.

"Leave it alone, guys, she was trying new things, it'll grow back," said Travers.

"Well, that proves love is blind," said Jones. "Unfortunately for us, we're not!"

"Too bad it's summer," said Henry. "You could wear a toque and save us the sight."

Travers grumbled and went to grab a cup of coffee. It was going to be a long day for him. With yet, another report to prepare, Henry pressed the on button on the monitor and loaded paper into the printer. The dot-matrix printer had a personality of its own. The paper came in a continuous ream, perforated to tear in a standard sheet but with left and right wings with holes to match the printer's feed wheels. Any misfed or misaligned paper would cause lights to flash, beeping and a complete stop to the whole project. Once properly fed and reset the printer would enthusiastically jump into action by lining itself up and giving a cheerful ding. For the rest of the print job, it would grind its way left to right with a thumping noise at each extremity, bouncing back for a return. To him, it sounded like an old washing machine.

Henry kept his desk free of clutter, pens aligned in a row on the right, a black and a red, plus a pencil. Baskets for ins and outs, the stapler to the left. He knew immediately if someone had touched his stuff, he didn't mind a borrow if things were returned to their place immediately after use. In contrast, Travers' desk was a bit like his life, things everywhere, never sure of what supplies he had, and lunch wrappers on the corners. He had a collection of business cards and notes with phone numbers for past and current lady friends. Jones was somewhere in between, so Henry felt there was hope left for him.

At the end of the day, Henry turned off the heat under the glass coffee pot. They went through quite a lot of those glass decanters, either cracked or the bottom blackened with burnt-in coffee residue. Justin Bates, the IT technician came over to chat. He'd heard that the guys were having a tough time with this investigation. Henry mentioned a few low points in the week and not much to look forward to.

"Do you want to come to a meetup?" asked Justin. "It's Saturday night, a place in Morrisburg."

"What's a 'meetup'?" asked Henry.

"Oh, it's like a single's club, they get together in the church hall. There's drinks and music, and lots of women," said Justin. "Come on, it'll take your mind off things."

Henry had to think for a minute. He wasn't really in the mood or ready for this type of interaction. But then again, it wasn't a bad idea to have some sort of social life. After all, what could go wrong with a few singles in a church hall…"Sure, what time?"

"Starts at 8 p.m.," said Justin. "We can each take our own car. It makes things easier if either of us meets someone nice. You know what I mean."

After that comment, Henry almost cancelled the whole thing, but for once he was going to stretch his comfort zone. This is what life was all about, he was turning a new leaf. Of course, on the day of, things were looking quite a bit scarier and all courage had left him.

He dressed in new pants and a shirt but wasn't sure if one did the jacket and tie. He opted for the jacket but not the tie. Combed his hair and for once he thought, the mug looking back at him in the mirror didn't look half bad. He drove to the address Justin had given him and noticed a full parking lot, with quite a few ladies going in. He didn't dare to get out of the car and waited for Justin to show up. There was security in numbers; he'd go in with him.

Justin pulled in beside his car and they walked up to the door. Henry noticed a sign that said "Parents without Partners Meeting"…

Henry pointed and asked Justin, "What's that?"

"That's the meetup, PWP, *Parents without Partners*," said Justin. "Most parents without partners are women, so lots come to these things."

"But…but I'm not a parent," said Henry.

"Doesn't matter, there's never enough men at these things, so they don't mind if someone brings a friend," explained Justin.

"You're kidding me," said Henry. He kept walking forward like a gladiator entering the arena to face the lions…or lioness, in this case.

Justin knew people here and waved at a young woman sitting with a couple of friends. He introduced Henry, who took a seat while Justin went for drinks. The ladies were good-looking, and nicely dressed, if a bit provocative to Henry's taste. Michelle, a kindergarten teacher was sitting next to Henry and quickly started the conversation. She had short brown hair, a pleasant face and nice curves, Henry noticed. But she must have been under thirty, a bit young for him. She asked what he did for a living and was quite taken by his police work. Henry was trying to ignore the red lights and bells that were flashing and ringing in his ears, he'd been down this path before.

The music started, a mix of line dancing, disco and slow dances. The lights were dimmed when slow dances came on. Henry figured Michelle liked him well enough because she touched him when they spoke and sat close to him. He asked her to dance to a disco tune and stayed on the dance floor when the music changed and the lights dimmed.

Being a gentleman, Henry thought it appropriate to keep a bit of daylight between him and his partner. Michelle felt otherwise. Henry was not completely immune to her charms, but he felt a bit awkward. *Heaven* by Bryan Adams, lasted four minutes, long enough for Michelle to ask if Henry had brought his handcuffs. At the end of the song, Henry excused himself.

Coming out of the washroom, he was approached by a tall blonde who said she thought her car had a flat tire and asked Henry if he minded having a look. They went out to the parking lot and it turned out the car was fine. The blonde laughed, thanked him and asked if he wanted to sit in her car and chat for a while. Henry declined. He needed a drink.

"Fancy meeting you here," said a voice he recognized. "Do you have your car?"

"Not you too…" said Henry as he turned and glanced at Lisa. She looked like he felt. "Do you want to get out of here?

"I thought you would never ask," said Lisa. On his way out he stopped by his table and said there was a police emergency, he needed to go. Michelle slipped her phone number in his hand. Justin thought Henry had picked up the woman he was talking to at the bar and gave him a thumbs up.

"Lucky escape," said Lisa. "What are you doing here?"

"A guy from work suggested this, I can't believe it. Now I know how produce feels, I felt like a tomato being squeezed for freshness. You?"

"Same, a friend from work," sighed Lisa. "From my point of view, there is way too much competition in there, did you see how many women there were?"

"I certainly did, and eager to say the least," and he went to explain the flat tire incident. "Talk about a *Parent without Partners* meeting."

"You know what they call these, right? I found out tonight, the guys call it *PWP, Pussies without Pricks* meetings!"

"No? Are you kidding me? Is this your first time there?" he laughed.

"First and last I believe," said Lisa. "But I understand the idea behind it. Most single parents are women and if you consider the limited time for dating, it's a quick solution to a common problem. Men are more than eager to oblige. I even heard of some not single at all."

"That's a shame," said Henry. "The ladies were smart and good-looking."

"Yes, but like I told you, with kids it's hard," added Lisa. "I've had guys come up to me and say I was nice enough, but they wouldn't date someone with kids. And for me, no man is going to make me regret having my kids. Not even Harrison Ford."

She turned and looked at him. "Anyone ever told you that you look a bit like Harrison Ford."

"Nope," grinned Henry.

"Not even your wife?"

"She called me many things but Harrison Ford was not one of them, I'd remember that. I guess she wanted to keep me humble."

They laughed and talked about Ellie and Jeremy all the way back to Winchester. It was Ellie's birthday next week and Lisa said Henry was welcome to drop in for a piece of cake. Henry literally couldn't wait to see Justin Bates back at the office on Monday.

On Sunday, Henry with Jeremy's help got back to boat building. As things progressed, they were encountering problems, one of them being space to work around the structure. It was fifteen feet one inch long, and four feet three inches wide. Once completed it would weigh two hundred and seventy-five pounds. The blueprint and instructions he had purchased from the used bookstore dated from 1933 had estimated the cost of building to $75, dream on thought Henry, he'd already spent $40 just getting the blueprint. Fifteen feet didn't seem that big on paper, but once it was raised on the trestles, you had to squeeze around it to store the wood pieces and the tools.

There were only ten boards in the hull, so easy enough. The men had spent time deciphering the jargon and terminology in the plans and information which were written by a down-easter. A small note in the body of the instructions now caught their attention, "Bear in mind that the projected transom on the body plan is not the transom to build"...There was something there about expansion and depth, which would keep Henry and Jeremy off the water for a while longer. The only instructions that seemed straightforward were the painting and buffing. At any rate, it was keeping them busy and took Henry's mind off his work.

"We should have read the instructions to the end," said Jeremy.

"We're men, we don't read instructions or ask for directions. Remember that," said Henry.

Chapter 17

Justin Bates was the first one to greet Henry when he came to work. The one person Henry hoped to avoid for as long as possible.

"Had a good time on Saturday?" asked Bates.

"It was all right," said Henry. He had kept Michelle's number. Would he ever consider calling her? He couldn't say for sure.

"Let me know if you want to do it again," said Bates. Travers joined in the conversation and Bates told him all about the *PWPs*. Travers showed great interest.

Jones provided the interruption Henry was looking for. There was some news on the McNeill's.

"We have some credit card activity in Ottawa," said Jones. "It's from a card belonging to Hugh McNeill, used Saturday night."

"Obviously, couldn't be Hugh McNeill, he was dead by then," commented Henry. "Do you think the killer stole his wallet?"

"Could be, or it could be Alex McNeill," said Jones. "The Ottawa boys are looking into it."

"Let me know once you have anything," said Henry. "Do you think Alex would show up here, for his father's funeral?"

"Could be, depends if he is guilty of anything, or just scared or confused," said Jones. "I'll ask for extra plain clothes officers, to be around at the service. Let me know when that is."

"Yes, I'll be talking to Mrs McNeill, I just wanted to give her some time to deal with the news," Henry added. "I'll talk to Joan again, she's the one who has been more forthcoming so far. That family has secrets."

When Henry went by *Treasures to Share* the shop was closed. He drove to the house and Joan was on her way out, she was going to stay with Evelyn for a few days.

"I'm sorry to bother you, Joan," said Henry. "Could we talk for a minute?"

Joan nodded and offered him a seat on the veranda. "I'm going to Winchester, to be with Evelyn. I can't open the shop, I'm not sure if I ever will now. And Evelyn needs someone, she's falling apart."

"A very difficult time for all of you," said Henry. "Have you heard anything from Alex?"

"No, not a thing and that's surprising," said Joan. "He was close to Mary; he was very affected by her death."

"He helped out in the shop, he told me," added Henry.

"It was more than that," said Joan. "You already know the situation with Hugh and Evelyn. Alex was also part of it. When things were bad at home, Hugh scaring him, he would often take refuge here. He'd go to work with Mary, he loved her dearly."

"It would help clear matters if he came back," said Henry. "Whether he did anything at all, it's better for him to own up to it. Right now, people are assuming too much."

"Oh, I know he would never have hurt Mary," said Joan. "And as for Hugh, although I don't wish death on anyone, and especially the way he went, I can't say I'm crying over him."

"You have my number, once you are at Evelyn's do call me if you hear from Alex," said Henry. "Did you discuss any plans for the funeral?"

"Given how it happened, Evelyn doesn't want a big public service. It will be something intimate, just the family, although now that is smaller than it used to be. Our father is aged and not in good health, he can't deal with this very well."

Henry touched her arm and they left together. Driving past the antique shop Henry noticed the "Sorry, we're closed" sign in the window. He knew then that he missed Mary Blake. She had been uncomplicated and carefree, she enjoyed life. He missed her affection, the smell of her hair, her hands. He could have used a hug, just about now.

On his way back Henry stopped at the construction site for the new development southeast of Winchester. Charles Brown Contractor was the builder here and there had been in-fighting between him and Hugh McNeill.

The construction trailer and office were at the entrance to the developments. Several large homes were already standing with more under various phases of construction. There was a steady flow of workers and visitors and Henry found Charles Brown looking at blueprints. Henry introduced himself and the reason for his visit.

"Hugh McNeill was your realtor for this project?" asked Henry.

"Yes, but I cancelled his contract after a few builds," said Brown. "We didn't see eye-to-eye on contracts and sales."

"And did you have words or was that a mutual parting?" added Henry.

"No, I gave him the exclusive to sell the lots and homes, but he made promises to sell more and that didn't work out," said Brown.

"Did he put you in some financial trouble? I imagine him losing the contract was hard?" asked Henry.

"Yes, for him it did hurt business, but he made promises to potential buyers that I couldn't carry out," explained Brown. "That put me in a bind."

"Can you give me an example?" said Henry.

"Well, he told some people that no one would build behind their lot, which was wrong. I can't leave open spaces everywhere. He promised a park, some upgrades in the interior, stuff like that."

"Did you come to blows? Did you threaten him in any way?"

"It wasn't pretty when customers started to tell me I had to do this and that because of McNeill. And to be honest with you, Hugh had a temper. He didn't take me telling him off any better than I did."

"Where were you last Tuesday, around 9 p.m.?" asked Henry.

"I was at home with the wife and kids. Probably with the oldest one finishing homework."

"Thank you very much for your time, Mr Brown, I know you are a busy man."

The final stop of the day was at the toy store, picking up something for Ellie's birthday tonight.

Today Ellie is six years old. She ran to Henry when he came into the yard, looking with interest at the gift wrap package he had in his hand. It was just the four of them tonight. Lisa had planned a bigger party with friends from kindergarten on Saturday.

"Happy birthday, Ellie," said Henry as he kissed her cheek and gave her the present.

"Thank you, Henry," she said. Not standing on ceremony, the paper was off the gift in seconds and she yelled with pleasure at the package.

It was a bit of an odd gift for a girl, Henry had first wondered, but he thought it would be a link between them. He had bought her a police officer set, or more a meter maid set, complete with a hat, a badge, handcuffs, a whistle, and a set of tickets for violations. Ellie took everything apart and came running back to Henry.

"Where's the gun? Henry, I need a gun?" she asked.

"No gun, baby. But nice that you bought my daughter handcuffs," laughed Lisa.

"You don't need a gun," said Henry. "See, you wear the hat and the badge and when someone does something bad you give them one of those small tickets. You can use the handcuffs if they don't listen."

"What do they do with the tickets?" asked Ellie.

"There is a fine, so they pay you money, and you take the ticket back," explained Henry.

Ellie figured it all out quickly, hoping for a gold mine from their bad behaviour. "I'm a policeman like you," she said showing her badge.

"You can be a policewoman, and we can work together," laughed Henry.

Ellie blew out her candles and enjoyed her cake and the rest of her presents from her Mom and Jeremy. Lisa couldn't stop laughing when Henry ended up in handcuffs.

Chapter 18

The ballistic results came in on Friday. The bullets that hit Hugh McNeill and the jerrycan full of fuel were a match for the one retrieved from the car stolen on that Sunday and left in the parking lot of the funeral home. A match for the one that had gone through Alex McNeill and was fired by Jerry Murphy. A perfect match from the gun that was still missing, stolen from Mary Blake. Once again, Henry Stafford did not hold the winning ticket…

Henry learned from Joan that Hugh McNeill's body had been released and that they would hold a small service on Monday afternoon. It would be followed by a private burial, here in Winchester. The family was trying to be as discreet as possible, their grief private as they could. Henry notified Jones so that he could get the extra plain clothes constables to monitor the event in case Alex made an appearance. He also asked Jones to get Jerry Murphy back in, since the bullet was now a match for the gun he held. In the first interview, he claimed the firearm was given back to Alex, but it was hearsay only. They desperately needed that gun and Alex McNeill.

Staff Sergeant Glenn called Henry in his office at the end of the day. He was anxious for progress and there was none.

"Slower than molasses climbing a hill in winter," said Glenn. "You guys are not coming up with anything, we're adding bodies and missing persons, not finding killers. What do you have to say, Stafford?"

"I believe that the key to all this is Alex McNeill," reflected Henry. "The fact that he has not been seen since the day his father died, is most strange, especially if he has nothing to hide."

"A person can't stay underground forever, especially at that age," said Glenn. "He's not a career criminal, doesn't have the connections and will need money at some point."

"Are you suggesting someone is helping him stay away," asked Henry. "His mother, his aunt?"

"You tell me, you're closer to them than I am. But if I were you, I'd follow that idea, look at phone calls, or quiet meetings."

"Yes, that might be a way to go," said Henry. He didn't like to be found at fault, but he could use all the help anyone could throw his way."

"The funeral is Monday," said Henry. "It might be hard for him to stay away, but I'll start keeping a closer eye on the mother and the aunt. Thanks."

Henry asked Travers to set up surveillance of Evelyn McNeill and Joan Blake. They also needed to investigate the phone calls they were making and receiving. This action, as small as it was, gave Henry some hope for a resolution.

When Jones told Henry there had been more activity on the Hugh McNeill credit card, their suspicions fell on Evelyn McNeill as the one covering for Alex. She had not reported the card missing, it had not been cancelled. With the card still active, statements would be sent to the house and those charges would show up. If Evelyn knew about them and did not flag them as suspicious, then she knew it was Alex using the card. Before leaving for the day, Henry told the dispatcher to call him, should any report come in from the surveillance of Evelyn and Joan. And that at any time over the weekend. Henry saw a faint light at the end of the tunnel.

Ellie came over just after supper to show Henry her new bike. Her father had gotten her a two-wheeler with training wheels. She wanted Henry to install her new bell on the handle. Lisa found Henry sitting in a folding chair just at the edge of his garage with a letter in his hand. He was slumped forward with his elbows on his knees, his eyes looking in the distance. He realized Lisa was standing beside him when Ellie called the cats over to her.

"What's up, Henry? Anything the matter?" asked Lisa. She pulled another folding chair beside his.

"Letter from my wife, Paula," said Henry. "She's asking for a divorce. I received it earlier this week. I made an appointment with a lawyer. I was just reading her letter again."

"Well, that's a good thing, isn't it? I thought it was over between the two of you," she said.

"It's not the divorce itself. Honestly, I couldn't care less," sighed Henry. "It's what she wants that bothers me. Money and a share of my police pension."

"Can you spare any money to give her what she wants?" She didn't know anything about his finances but assumed he'd been in this house a long time and didn't seem to have extravagant expenses on a good salary.

"Not as much as I could have a few months ago," said Henry very slowly, he was going to admit to something he had kept to himself up to now.

"I bought the house next door, your house…"

"What? Oh, Henry, you shouldn't have. We would have managed," said Lisa.

"I know, but I didn't want the kids to go," and he smiled, "It was an investment anyway. It's a good house and the price was right."

"So, what's the financial strain?" she was curious.

"I had $40,000 in Canada Savings Bonds, and I was going to use that to buy the house, only when I went to find them, I realized Paula had taken the lot," he said evenly. "I ended up having to mortgage it and the rates are high now."

"So, she wants half of both houses and your police pension? You have to fight that, Henry."

"No, I'll find a way," he said resigned in his typical fashion.

"But that's not right, especially if she already took the bonds from you, that should be included in what she gets, and besides she was unfaithful and SHE left you," she said as though she was the offended party.

"I'll figure it out," said Henry. He looked up at her and finally noticed that she was all dressed up, with make-up and all the works.

"You're looking great. Going anywhere special?" he asked.

"Yes, I have a date, with Wes, an ambulance driver," said Lisa. "He's been asking me out for a while and I finally said yes."

"You have more courage than I…but that's great," said Henry, with fake enthusiasm. "I hope you have a great time." Which was true, well, not really. He secretly hoped the guy smelled like garlic and had small feet…because he knew what they said about the size of a guy's feet and the size of his….

"I'll put the bell on Ellie's bike then," said Henry.

"I hope we can talk about this divorce business again Henry," said Lisa. "Fight it."

Chapter 19

The pager went off at 11:35 p.m. on Saturday. Henry had just gone to bed. "Why couldn't people do bad things during business hours?" he muttered. They had a sighting of a young man, who had entered the McNeill house from the side door of the garage. Henry got dressed and drove over. He saw the unmarked car parked down the street and went to talk to the constable. According to him, the man, tall and slim, young and dressed in jeans and a t-shirt, entered the garage but he had not seen him leave. Henry called for backup. He didn't want to risk losing him and there was still the small matter of a handgun missing.

Henry sent one officer to watch the back and garage side door, while the other stayed in his car. Henry rang the bell first and knocked heavily on the front door when there was no answer. Evelyn McNeill finally opened the door.

"Listen, Evelyn, we know Alex is here," said Henry. "Don't make this any more difficult than it already is. We need him to come in and answer questions."

"His father's funeral is on Monday," cried Evelyn. "Can't you leave us alone until then?"

"Unfortunately, I can't do that," explained Henry. "He's a flight risk now. There is a missing handgun, we need to clear this up, one way or another. Please, Evelyn, you don't want to get yourself in trouble by covering for him."

She opened the door wide and let him in. Alex was standing at the top of the stairs. Henry signalled the constable to come in and take Alex to the station.

"We'll take him in now. I would advise getting him a lawyer," said Henry.

Alex did not say a word at any time during his arrest. They processed him and took him to a holding cell. Henry knew he had work ahead of him because any good lawyer would try to get his client out on bail as soon as he could. In theory, Alex was a missing person, but there were gun and car thefts. At this time, they had no motive or witnesses to place him at his father's murder. It was a mess. They could hold him for twenty-four hours because they had probable cause. Also, and this being a weekend, they had until Monday night. Henry also faced a moral dilemma. Monday afternoon was the funeral for the boy's father. Right now, Henry considered letting him attend, accompanied by two plainclothes officers. But what if the young man was involved in his father's demise? Henry would need to see what transpired over the next day.

After another short night, Henry was slow to get moving on this Sunday morning. He expected to be called in again, to deal with any progress with Alex McNeill. Out of milk and bread, he walked up to the corner store for supplies. By now it was time for brunch more than breakfast, so he fired up the grill with the griddle and threw on bacon, potatoes and eggs. If he had to go back to work at least he'd go on a full stomach. Coffee in hand, Henry glanced at the business card from the divorce lawyer he had found in the yellow pages of the phone book. Henry didn't want to deal with any of it, but Lisa was right. As much as he wanted to be fair and give Lisa her due, she had already taken $40,000. For him to have to re-mortgage or even sell both houses and lose half of his pension would seriously impact his financial future. Paula had quit her job as a secretary as soon as they married. Henry thought it was ideal should they have children; she would be home for them. But none had come, and she never showed interest in going back to work. She had left him, with only a note. It was time she made her own way or got Edgar to carry the load.

Of course, Henry's career wasn't over, he had been in twenty years now, so there were ten more to go before retirement. He could be transferred to a larger centre, get a promotion and more money, but he never planned for that. After graduation, the opening in Winchester came up and he applied for it. He loved the idea of a small town and community policing. Winchester was less than an hour from Ottawa and close to Morrisburg and Cornwall, which gave him access to the waterfront. Winchester's population was about sixteen hundred and it suited him fine. Enough stores and restaurants for what he needed. Paula had not felt the same though, and he realized this more now. He knew that she would have preferred a larger city, but she had access to a car so she managed well. To Henry, a small town would have been an ideal place to raise kids. He also loved Sunday drives exploring the Counties, again something Paula did not enjoy. Bottom line it seemed, they had little in common, except for the chequing account.

The phone rang bringing Henry back to reality. Alex McNeill had a lawyer who wanted to meet and go over details with his client. Henry confirmed he was on his way, changed and walked up the street to the station. Alex looked rough; the night had been short for him as well. In these austere surroundings and a tough situation, Henry guessed he hadn't slept at all. David Paul was the lawyer; Henry knew him and he was a reasonable man.

"Hi Alex, how are you doing?" started Henry. "I don't know if you remember me, but I'm Detective Sergeant Henry Stafford." Alex nodded but didn't say a word.

"Listen, Alex, I know things have been difficult for you, and I'm not here to make them more complicated," said Henry. "I would very much like to help you sort this out, okay?" Alex looked up at him and nodded again.

"Can you tell us where the gun is? It would help to get it off the streets," asked Henry. "The one you stole from your aunt. We already know it was the weapon used to kill your father."

"It's in the glove compartment of my car," admitted Alex. "But I didn't shoot him."

"And where is your car now," asked Henry.

"It's at my mother's house, in the garage," said Alex.

"Where were you last Tuesday evening, between 8 and 9 pm?" asked Henry.

"I was at home, I had come across Jerry Murphy, around supper time. My father had hit him and I went straight home to see my mother."

"I know your mother went to Chesterville, to your Aunt Joan, that evening, but you didn't go with her?" asked Henry. "What happened, what did you do instead?"

Alex looked scared; the same look Henry had noticed when he talked about his father before. That physical fear coming from the young man.

"I told my mother what happened between my father and Jerry Murphy," said Alex. "She was upset about it. She told me to stay home and she took off. She came back around 11:30 that evening, told me what happened at the store and that she had been with Aunt Joan."

"When did you leave Winchester?" asked Henry. "We have a missing person's report for you and some credit card activity in Ottawa."

Henry saw Alex hold back the tears, thinking back on the events. "I left right then and there, I was upset. I told my mother I would stay with friends for a while. But I didn't tell her where or which friends."

"But later you must have contacted your mother, she knew where you were and covered for you?" asked Henry. Alex nodded.

"On that Tuesday night, did you try to follow your mother after she left?" asked Henry. "You didn't go to Chesterville later?"

"How could I," said Alex. "My parents have only one car and my father had it. My mother took my car, I was stranded at home until she came back."

Interesting thought Henry, that statement changed the direction of the investigation in a major way. "Did your mother know that the gun was in your car?" asked Henry.

"Yes, I told her, a while back," said Alex. "I told her I wanted to bring it back to the store. She said she would take care of it for me."

Henry now knew that Evelyn had gone to Chesterville before the murder and fire. She had been on her way to see Joan, with a gun in the car. He wondered if Joan also knew where the gun was. The sisters were starting to piss him off. This was amounting to obstruction of justice. Covering up for each other and knowingly withholding information about the weapon.

Alex's lawyer, David Paul, spoke up for the first time. "Tomorrow is my client's father's funeral. We had hoped he could attend. Out of respect for the family and this difficult situation."

"Yes," said Henry. "I had considered this. This afternoon I will send for proper clothing for him, and on Monday send two plainclothes officers with Alex. Given that consideration, I would expect cooperation from your client, there and back. Agreed?"

David Paul looked at Alex, who agreed and thanked DS Stafford. Alex returned to his holding cell.

"We will talk again," said Henry.

Henry was annoyed. The point of all this had been to try and find who killed Mary Blake. Now the McNeill family saga was draining all the oxygen out of the room. To him, the security guard, Russell Davis, did not hold water as the killer. So now, someone in the McNeill family was circling the drain. Enough is enough, he called Jones in and he arranged to bring in Evelyn McNeill and Joan Blake for questioning. He sent a team to search the car in the hope of finding the firearm.

Within half an hour of being back in his cell, Alex McNeill asked to see DS Stafford again. Alex was distraught and nervous. Henry brought him a can of pop from the vending machine.

"It's all a mess," said Alex. "I can't deal with it anymore; I want my life back."

"Do you want me to call your lawyer back in? asked Henry.

"No, it won't make a difference now."

"Ok, so tell me what happened," said Henry. "Tell us the truth, which is the only way out of this, Alex. And you know it."

"On that Monday, when my Aunt Mary died," he started. "I went with my father to the shop in Chesterville."

"And what time was that?" asked Henry.

"It was in the morning, we got there around 10 am," said Alex. "I wanted to go with him because I thought I could put the gun back in the case that was below the cash register. But when I got there my father told me to stay in the car. I got out anyway and was going to go in the front since my father and Aunt Mary were talking in the back office."

"Did you hear what they were talking about?" asked Henry.

"Yes, when I got out of the car, it was parked by the back door," said Alex. "I heard them arguing about selling property, and then my father made a move for her and he said, 'You're screwing everyone else, so why not me?' so I went to the front hoping to get in but I saw a large man coming out of the shop."

"And what did you do?"

"I moved out of sight and saw Aunt Mary come to the front, probably because she heard the bell over the door," explained Alex. "My father followed her and they argued, he pushed her and she fell backwards. I got scared and went back to the car, I thought my father was going to phone for help or something, but no, he just ran back to the car and took off."

"Did he know you saw him?" asked Henry

"No, but he told me not to say a word about us being in Chesterville that morning," cried Alex.

"And you didn't say anything to anyone?" asked Henry.

"No, when my father gives you an order, you shut up or pay up," said Alex. "That's what I learned. So, I put the gun back in my car and left it there."

"Just to be clear, you never told anyone, at any time, about what you saw?" pushed Henry.

"Finally, I did tell my mother, on that Tuesday, the day my father was killed," said Alex. Tears were running down his face and he was shaking.

"It's ok Alex. We'll get through this, it will feel a lot better once everything is out in the open," said Henry. "Keeping secrets is draining after a while. Keep going."

"After my father beat up my friend, I knew he was coming after me, and I was fed up with his abuse," confided Alex. "I told my mother I had seen him, argue and push Aunt Mary, probably killing her and not even trying to help her. I've seen everything he did to my mother and I had enough."

"And what did your mother do then?"

"She was upset, she cried and finally she said it was enough. She took my car. I had already told her I couldn't put the gun back and that it was still in the car, that's when she told me she would look after it." By now young Alex was sobbing. Henry thanked him for admitting all this. Alex went back to his cell.

Chapter 20

"I'm sorry to drag you in on a Sunday but I want to get this over with," said Henry to Jones who just walked in the station. He quickly filled him in on what Alex had confessed to and that they were waiting for Joan and Evelyn to be brought in for questioning.

"I'll talk to Evelyn McNeill and you can take Joan Blake," said Henry.

"Did you get anything out of the car? The gun?" asked Jones.

"No, and that's the problem. Where is it now?" asked Henry. "We know that Evelyn McNeill went to Chesterville with Alex's car and the gun was in the glove compartment. Did she stop on her way by the antique shop or did she go directly to Joan?"

"One of them, must have killed Hugh McNeill," said Jones.

"It certainly looks that way. And Evelyn knew he had killed her sister by then. What a mess. I'm not crazy about them covering for each other and Alex. It doesn't build trust!"

David Paul, McNeill's lawyer came back again to the station, this time he stood with Evelyn McNeill.

Henry went in with them and Jones waited for Joan Blake to arrive.

Evelyn McNeill played the offended grieving widow, asking why she was brought in the day before her husband's funeral. "Surely, this is a joke, you already have Alex in custody, what are you trying to do to us?" she asked.

"New information has come to light Mrs McNeill and it turns out you might not have been forthcoming with me," said Henry. She had just reached the end of his rope.

"Do you know where the gun is?" asked Henry. "Alex said he told you about it and that it was in the glove compartment of his car. But when we checked it wasn't there, so where is it?"

"I gave it to Joan, for safekeeping and so that she may put it back in its place in the shop," said Evelyn.

"Mrs McNeill, do you take me for an idiot?" asked Henry. She gave him the most innocent smile she could. "You knew we were looking for that gun from the start, and now we know it's the weapon used to kill your husband. Yet, you handle it like it's a borrowed handkerchief, with no words said."

"We can take fingerprints, but the firearm has been touched by everyone, perhaps a smart move to cover the guilty party," said Henry.

"How can you say this?" sighed Evelyn. "My family is in disarray, my husband dead, my son in jail."

"Yes, and I'm sorry for that," said Henry. "But you have been lying, covering for Alex and who knows what else. The games are over. I know that you went to Chesterville, on Tuesday evening, with access to a weapon. So, it's very possible you stopped by the antique shop, saw your husband and fired at him. Care to go over the story one more time?"

"No, I didn't stop at the shop, I went straight to Joan," said Evelyn. "I needed to confide in her, so she could help me. Now that I knew Hugh had killed Mary, I just couldn't bear it alone."

"You went to Joan and then what?"

"We talked for a while and we heard the sirens and the noise. As you know her house is just down from the shop," said Evelyn. "We went over to see what had happened; we thought the shop was on fire. And that was it, you saw us there later."

"Did you bring the gun in with you, in the house, to give it to Joan," asked Henry.

"No, I was very upset and forgot about it," cried Evelyn.

"So in between you getting to Joan's house and your husband being shot, how did the gun get from the glove compartment to the parking lot behind the shop?" asked Henry. If he wasn't so angry, he would be smiling at the creativity this woman employed.

"It was probably stolen from the car, in between me going in the house and Hugh getting shot," tried Evelyn. "I left the car door unlocked, as you always do in a small town, and it's only a short walk from the house to the shop."

"You're telling me, with a straight face to boot, that out of sheer coincidence, a total stranger got to the car, opened the glove compartment at random, found a gun and went directly to the antique shop to shoot your husband? For what reason?"

"You know as well as I do that there are bad people out there, Detective Stafford," said Evelyn. She looked at her lawyer, smiled and nodded.

"I must excuse myself; I will be back in a few minutes. I need to see if your sister Joan has arrived," said Henry. He glanced at her and saw her annoyance. "Yes, the gang's all here and no one is going home until we figure this out. Make yourself comfortable, your lawyer can get you tea or coffee."

"And Mister Paul, if I were you, I would advise your client on obstruction of justice as a start," said Henry. "I wouldn't call you a liar Mrs McNeill, but you have been very creative with your interpretation of events. For example, when you reported Alex missing, you had just seen him at your house, and you borrowed his car to go to Chesterville. You wasted police time and misled us in this enquiry."

Henry went to pour himself a cup of coffee, he would let her simmer for a while. The woman should be writing for the summer theatre, her imagination was unbelievable, in all senses of the word. Henry called Jones out of the interview room and related what Evelyn had told her. Jones had a good laugh.

A call to Staff Sergeant Glenn was in order. Henry had the whole McNeill and Blake families in interviews. He had suspicions about two of them, and Alex was a witness to Mary Blake's murder. Russell Davis would now be cleared and good to release. But still, he had no murder weapon and no witnesses or confessions. Some things were just above his pay grade, and the funeral was tomorrow afternoon. He apologized for disturbing his superior on a Sunday, but he needed confirmation. If they didn't let the family go to the funeral, the media might have a field day about this, especially if they couldn't prove any of them were guilty of the murder. He quickly brought Staff Sergeant Glenn up to date.

"Have you discussed this with DI Rowley?" asked Glenn.

"I can't find him anywhere, perhaps you should have a go at it?" suggested Stafford.

"Ok then," said Glenn. "Let Alex McNeill and the rest of the family go to the funeral but have officers there."

"I will continue the questioning afterwards," said Stafford.

"May I suggest you put pressure on one of them, forcing either a confession or at least a break in their resolve to protect one another," said Glenn.

Henry told Jones to let Joan go but to caution her about leaving town, he would do the same with Alex and Evelyn. They would start this again after the funeral. He dragged himself back to his house and thought that if this kept up, he'd never make it to his fiftieth birthday. He'd swear his new pants were now also too big. He'd been too distracted to snack or take comfort in a glazed doughnut. He sat outside with a beer, enjoying whatever was left of his weekend. He saw Lisa coming up the stairs to the patio.

"My god, you look in bad shape, sorry!" said Lisa. "This investigation is getting hard on you, isn't it?" Henry nodded and he didn't know what to say, he'd never been asked to share much of his days in the past and caring interest was new to him.

"I have a letter for you, it was in my mailbox by mistake," said Lisa. "I'm sorry, it must have come Friday, but I just went through the mail today. There's normally never anything interesting, just bills." She gave him the envelope. "It's from the Museum in Scotland, the one you wrote about the military photos."

Henry had almost forgotten about that. But come to think of it, with Russell Davis cleared, he might just get his box back. He opened the letter and smiled, "They are interested, they say they would pay postage."

"That's good news for you then," said Lisa. "Can I tell Jeremy? I'm sure he will be interested."

Henry remembered that Lisa went out on a date Saturday night. "So how was your date?"

"Let's just say it was a one-off," laughed Lisa. "There won't be a repeat. I'm done."

"What happened? If you don't mind me asking."

"We drove around for a bit and Wes took me to a restaurant in Morrisburg because he wanted to use his coupons. Later we went to the waterfront to see the boats come in. He said he'd invite me over to his house but he lives with his mother."

"Ouch," laughed Henry. "There's more?"

"Oh, yes, he got ice cream from the park vendor, he had two-for-one coupons for that too. At the waterfront, he kept reaching into his glove compartment, for a cassette tape, or a napkin, always finding a way to brush against me. Later he wanted to get a bit closer so we could get to know each other better."

"Creep," said Henry. "What did you do?"

"I told him it was a lovely evening but I had to get home, I was just too worried about the kids to relax," grinned Lisa.

"Good for you," said Henry. "I'm sorry it didn't work out." And he meant it this time, they were friends and he wanted good things to happen to her. Henry knew he would never ask her out. He liked how things were going now, they had a good routine. Anything more would imply a risk and Henry had always avoided risk like Dracula avoided garlic.

"Did you hear any more from your lawyer? When is the meeting?" she asked.

"This Wednesday, I have a good lawyer, and since Paula is still in Saskatchewan, there is a lawyer representing her. She won't be coming," explained Henry. "It shouldn't take long, since we don't have any children to fight over, it's just money."

"Fight Henry, I'll go with you," she said firmly. "Give me the time and place and I'll be there to support you."

Henry thought about it and realized he could count on one hand, while not using too many fingers, the number of times anyone had wanted to "support" him. It was unfamiliar territory, risky even.

"Ok, it's at Dennis Wells' office on Main, you know besides the drugstore, I'm on at 9:30 in the morning.

"I'll be there," said Lisa.

Henry watched her walk away and chastised himself for the thoughts that were going through his mind, but it reminded him he was alive, lonely, and a coward.

Chapter 21

Once again Henry, Jones and Travers found themselves sitting in the back pew of a United Church. This time in Winchester, on St. Lawrence Street. Travers was now sporting a very short hairstyle, the result of cutting even more off the sides to even off the cut. He was going to live with the eyebrows for a while longer. The trim ended up giving him a steady perplexed look that Henry and Jones were growing used to.

Plainclothes constables, and DI Rowley amongst them, were keeping an eye on Alex, Evelyn and Joan. The service was so private and small that there were more police present than family and friends. The service was restricted to a few members of the McNeill family, a few close friends and the only remaining members of the Blake family on Evelyn's side. It had been a cremation and later the urn would be given back to Evelyn and Alex to go in the columbarium.

"I hope she got a discount," whispered Travers. "He was already half done."

Henry kicked him back into silence. He flipped through a Church Bulletin, folded it, and put it in his pocket. Henry looked at Alex, Joan and Evelyn and thought that one of them was a good actor. His gut feeling was that one of them killed Hugh McNeill. But who of the grieving widow, the supportive sister or the accusing son was in line for the Academy Award?

After the short service, there was coffee in the Church Hall and it was sparsely attended. Overall, it was awkward and people didn't know what to say. Travers didn't miss taking a plate of those small triangular sandwiches and a few cookies. Now, they would bring the whole gang back to the station and start the interviews again.

Back at the station, Henry pulled the Church Bulletin out of his pocket. It had given him an idea. On the Tuesday night of Hugh McNeill's murder, they interviewed the neighbours. The parking at the back of the antique shop bordered on a property but it was hidden by trees. The shop and restaurant were on a corner lot at King and Water streets. The parking lot for the businesses was L-shaped and accessible from both streets. The restaurant next to the antique shop closed at 7 p.m. and the events occurred around 9 p.m., at dusk. The parking lot and the back door had some lighting. No one had seen anything. The next street behind King was Casselman and on the corner was Christ Church United, one way to access the Church was via Water Street.

When Henry had looked at the Church bulletin, he noticed evening meetings. He wondered if similar events happened at Christ Church and if anyone, not a neighbour but a participant, might have seen something. Some might even have parked on Water

Street walking past the parking lot on their way to the Church. He called the minister and explained the situation. He was aware of the sad events and was eager to help. He said most Church related functions happened during the day but some groups used the Church Hall for meetings in the evenings. He would look at the bookings for that Tuesday and pass the word around that the police were looking for anyone who might have seen something, anything. Henry gave him his phone number and told him that even the smallest detail could be helpful.

They had found Hugh McNeill's car on Casselman Street. He had walked to the back of the shop. It was unlikely he carried a gas can from there to the back door. Did he drop off the fuel, park the car further down and come back with plans to burn the shop? Two gunshots were fired and instantly the fire started. The neighbours claimed they heard the shots but were more taken by the fire and called emergency services at once. But someone had met Hugh McNeill and shot him. Did that person exit by foot or did a quick in and out in a car? Did no one see the car rushing out? As usual, when Henry went over the chain of events, there were always more questions than answers.

Once everyone was back at the station for the interrogation, they divided the tasks. The available space limited the number of interviews they could do at the same time. Henry would take Evelyn; Jones would talk to Joan and Travers would see if there was anything else they could find out from Alex. Henry briefed them on the strategy they were going to use to try and break this deadlock.

Henry asked Evelyn to go over her statement one more time. As he expected there were no changes to what she had claimed previously. She maintained someone must have stolen the gun from the car while she was at Joan's. Henry closed the interview sharply and thanked her for her help.

"Mrs McNeill, you can go now, but please remain available for any additional questions we might have," said Henry. She looked stunned.

"And what about Alex?' she asked. "Is he also free to go?"

"I'm afraid not," said Henry in his best poker face. "He was the last one with the gun, he had issues with his father beating up his friend and he saw him kill his aunt. And by all accounts, he cared for her very much. Motive, opportunity and means, it's all there."

"But…" started Evelyn.

"I'll have someone drive you home, you have my number if you remember anything else." Henry walked out.

Parallel events were unfolding for Jones when he talked to Joan. He told her she was free to go but they were keeping Alex. Travers was telling Alex he would stay a while because of gun charges and that his mother would be questioned further. Based on his statement, his mother was the last one to have the gun and she was on her way to Chesterville at the time of the murder. All three were speechless. Henry had cracked the eggs, now he was lighting the fire under the pan. He hoped his bluff would pay off, sooner than later. This investigation had interfered with his photo collecting, ruining a few weekends and slowing the progress he had been making on building the boat. He had not spent as much time with Ellie and Jeremy as he would have liked and that was irritating. He would give anything for a return to slow Mondays, those without murders.

Chapter 22

Lisa had agreed to go with Henry to see his divorce lawyer and support him so he could fight the settlement his wife was asking for. It had seemed a good idea at the time but now she was wondering whether she should have volunteered for it. After all, they weren't in a relationship - they were friends at best. Was she out of her reach? But again, they were friends and Henry didn't seem to have many of those, or family for that matter. He had been decent enough to buy the house she was renting so they wouldn't have to move. That was something huge. He was so good with the kids; she had come to care for him. But she also saw his limitations. There'd been many openings but he never said anything. She decided he didn't fancy her in that way, but the friendship was priceless. She would be there with him on Wednesday.

Lisa got ready for her evening shift, hoping it would be a quiet one. The pace of an emergency shift could go from zero to sixty in a few minutes. All you needed was a traffic accident involving multiple cars and the ambulances would be lining up at the door.

At the end of a quiet evening, with only a few babies with a fever and a senior who had fallen, Lisa thought about Henry. He never said much about his wife and she was curious. She knew she shouldn't do this, but she walked over to medical records and pulled Paula's file. Nothing much, routine visits for tests, and then she saw it. She looked closer at the date, the background and the follow-up. Oh, My God! But she couldn't use it, could she? It could mean her job!

The lawyer's office was as quiet as a church and just as formal. Heavy wooden panels and framed credentials on the wall decorated the waiting room. Lisa took a seat beside Henry, they smiled at each other, a bit awkwardly. Would it look bad to show up for a divorce settlement accompanied by another woman, thought Henry. Given that his wife had left with the next-door neighbour, he didn't think it mattered much.

The secretary ushered them into a conference room. Paula's lawyer was already sitting on the left, they took chairs on the right, beside Dennis Wells, his lawyer. The whole set-up was very confrontational, and that wasn't to Henry's liking at all.

Dennis introduced everyone, and Paula's lawyer, Robert Auger, presented his demands. It was as he remembered, half of everything including his police retirement pension. He sighed.

Wells presented a counterproposal. Auger looked offended at the offer of nothing but the

$40,000 in Canada Savings Bond she had taken with her when she left.

"Surely, you can do better than that," said Auger with a sardonic smile.

"I would like to remind you, Mr Auger, that Mrs Stafford was unfaithful before the marriage ended, and that she left the family home. The bonds would have also earned interest by the time Mrs Stafford cashed them," said Wells.

"Certainly, Mr Wells, but there is also a claim of mental cruelty from Mrs Stafford, she had no choice but to leave the home," added Auger.

"What?" said Stafford. This mental cruelty complaint was news to him, and untrue. He whispered something into his lawyer's ear.

"Mr. Auger, we would need documentation for this new assertion, some proof from your client, witnesses," said Wells and he continued, "From the point of view of Mr. Stafford, these claims are false and he would have witnesses to the contrary. Enough to substantiate a claim of his own for the same accusation."

Lisa took it all in and although she had not known Henry and Paula as a couple, there's been enough comments in the neighbourhood to paint quite a different picture. She knew mental abuse and Henry had never shown any of the patterns. She also reflected on what she had uncovered on Monday.

"May I speak with Mr Wells in private for a few minutes?" asked Lisa. They moved over to the side. Henry was puzzled by that request and had no clue what it was all about. Lisa went back to her seat and Wells called Henry over. There was a brief discussion and Henry went as white as a sheet as he shook his head.

"Very well," said Wells and they took their seat again.

"I have advised Miss Stuart against coming forward, as this could jeopardize her employment, but she insists," said Wells.

Wells continued, "Miss Lisa Stuart is a nurse at the Winchester General Hospital. She has come across some medical information regarding Mrs Stafford. A follow-up to a procedure obtained outside of the hospital seven years ago. I would advise you, Mr. Auger, to go back to your client and discuss this further. We have no interest in entering this information as evidence for our counterproposal, but if Mrs Stafford insists, we will. This is damaging to her, not to my client."

"At present, this meeting will be adjourned, with our proposal of a $40,000 settlement in Canada Savings Bond, already in the possession of your client," closed Wells. "Have a good day, Mr. Auger. I look forward to hearing from you so we can close this matter."

Paula's lawyer was taken aback and a bit in the dark about the last comments. Had his client withheld information? He gathered his papers, closed his briefcase and walked out.

Wells, Henry and Lisa stayed behind. Henry fell back in his chair.

"I had no idea," he said.

"I'm sorry Henry. I didn't want to hurt you and I wouldn't have said anything but I saw that the mental cruelty implications were unfair to you," said Lisa. "You have been good to me and the kids. I had to make it right."

"You didn't know your wife had an abortion seven years ago?" asked Wells.

Henry shook his head, he couldn't speak. How could he have not known? At that moment he thought of the times she had gone away for a few days, visiting her family. He was shaken, he felt like a hand was squeezing his heart. Did Paula have an abortion because she didn't want to have his child or because she was unfaithful even then? How could she go as far as blaming him for the infertility?

Lisa felt tears come to her eyes when she realized what she had done. She now understood Henry's reluctance to fight. In what mattered to him, not money and pensions, the cost of this settlement had just been much too high.

Wells hoped that a resolution would come without threatening Lisa's job. Her breach of confidentiality did not need to be made formal. If Paula Stafford realized she had more to lose than to gain now that Henry knew about the abortion, she would simply settle as recommended.

Henry and Lisa walked out of the office in silence.

"Do you need a ride back?" asked Henry.

"No, I drove," she said. "Henry, I'm so sorry, maybe I should have talked to you first…"

"It's all right Lisa. You did what you thought was best, it's in the past. Thank you," said Henry as he got into his car and back to work.

Head bowed, Henry Stafford, got off the Happiness Train. He desperately needed the break. He'd wait for the next train hoping for a better ticket on the last leg of the trip.

Chapter 23

If Wednesday morning had been an absolute disaster for Henry, at least the afternoon was shaping up better. Staff Sergeant Glenn had given him back his box of photos. Both the purchase and the sale had been legitimate and legal, supported with receipts. Henry was the rightful owner. He was anxious to tell Jeremy about it and prepare the military photos for shipping to the museum in Scotland.

Alex McNeill had not changed his story, so Henry felt confident he was telling the truth. The inquiry with the Chesterville Christ Church United had also paid off. A few people were coming in with information about a car they saw that night at the back of *Treasures to Share*. Jones had not come in today; his wife was in labour. Henry thought he'd have to get a gift for the baby.

Different reports came from the two people who had been at the Church Alcoholics Anonymous meeting on that Tuesday evening. The meeting had started at 7 p.m. and ended around 8:30 p.m. with a few stragglers staying behind to chat and clean up. One man, who left just before 9 pm saw a red Cutlass exit the parking lot on to Water Street then down to Casselman and park. The man got out of the car and walked back up the street. He was tall with a moustache. Another witness who left a few minutes later, went up Water and turned right on King Street. He was cut off by a woman who seemed in a hurry. She was driving a dark car, what looked like a brown Chevette. Both men lived out of town and said they didn't know about what happened after they left the meeting, so they didn't think to report anything.

That confirmed Henry's line of thinking that Hugh McNeill had dropped off the gas can, went to park and walked back up to the back door of the store. The Chevette was Alex's car driven, it seemed, by a woman. Possibly his mother went back to Joan's after shooting Hugh and setting the fire. What a mess. The clerk at the front called Henry to the reception area, two ladies, Mrs Blake and Mrs McNeill wanted to see him.

Henry offered them a coffee or tea and ushered them into the front interview room. He had grabbed a coffee for himself and was looking forward to their chat.

"Good Day, what can I do for you?" asked Henry.

"We would like to confess to Hugh McNeill's murder," said Joan.

Henry nearly choked on the sip of coffee he had taken. "What do you mean 'We'? Who did it?"

"We think both of us," said Evelyn.

"Care to just go through what happened, one thing after the other and we will figure this out," said Henry. Curiosity was getting the better of him. He stepped out and called Travers, so he could sit with him as a second witness to the confession. Before going into the room, he whispered to Travers "They both did it" and smiled.

"This is Detective Constable Travers, present as a second witness to the confession," said Henry. "Let's start at the beginning."

Evelyn started, "I saw Alex at our house, he told me about seeing Hugh push Mary and leaving her there. He told me about his father beating up his friend and I could see he was scared to death of him."

Her demeanour was different because she was in complete control of herself, unlike all the previous times when she had seemed so tensed and afraid. She was still fragile, but all fear had gone.

"Go on, please."

"I decided then and there that it was enough," said Evelyn. "Enough of being scared, pushed around and feeling hopeless. It wasn't that I was scared for myself anymore but for Alex. I knew what his father could do and it had to end. The boy needed to have a life, a future…"

"You took his car, knowing there was a gun in it," said Travers.

"Yes, I drove to Chesterville. There I saw Hugh's car pulling into the shop's parking lot. I wanted to confront him but I was too scared. I drove to Joan's which is just down the road. I shared all that I had learned from Alex and told her I saw Hugh at the store."

"I didn't know what he was doing at the shop, but for me, it wasn't good news," said Joan, who spoke for the first time. "I wanted to stop whatever he was doing. I wasn't going to stand for his bullying. I also had enough."

"It's ok Joan, you don't have to cover for me anymore," said Evelyn.

"For years, the only one who stood up to him was Mary and look where it got her," said Joan. "Me, I pretended to look the other way, when Evelyn had bruises or stayed home for a few days when he had pushed her down the stairs. And we were losing Alex in all of it."

"What happened after?" asked Henry.

"Joan decided to go to the store," said Evelyn. "We went together, I drove. When we got there, I pulled in the back and saw Hugh with a can, like the one we have for the lawnmower gasoline. It was clear what he was going to do."

"I got out of the car, but before I did, I grabbed the gun," said Joan. "I pointed it towards Hugh and told him to stop."

"He just laughed at us," said Evelyn in tears. "He laughed like we didn't matter much. He told me to get home and he'd look after me and Alex later. So, I thought 'No, not anymore.' I grabbed the gun from Joan, but she tried to take it back. As we wrestled the gun went off once and then again."

"The second time it hit the gas can and it exploded, spilt onto Hugh and it was horrible," said Joan. See - we were both holding the gun when it happened."

"But we were resolved to keep on going," said Evelyn. "We got back in the car, pulled away and turned around when the fire trucks pulled in, making it look like we just got there."

"Where is the gun now?" asked Henry.

Evelyn reached into her handbag and put the weapon on the desk. It was a Smith & Wesson 539, a 9mm with a magazine for eight rounds, with five remaining. Travers got an evidence bag and using his pen to pick it up, dropped it in. He didn't need to add his fingerprints to all those already on the gun. Alex, Joan and Evelyn had touched it already.

The two women were now huddled together, holding hands and in some way still protecting each other. Henry suggested they call their lawyer in so the police department could proceed with charges. Henry and Travers left the room. Henry reflected on their interactions since the beginning. They had played him for a fool. The missing person's report, the grief when he told Evelyn, all of it, was an act.

"What do you think boss?" asked Travers. "Could they have both done it? Surely one had a finger on the trigger or did they both, one after the other? It's puzzling."

"For sure," said Henry. "Accidental or did they intend to kill him? Hugh had threatened Evelyn. The unlucky bastard got two stray bullets, one in the heart and the other in the gas can. What are the odds?"

"One thing is clear, it absolves Alex of any wrongdoing, and perhaps that's what they wanted," said Travers. "When the shots were fired, it was Evelyn who was holding the gun, even if Joan was trying to take it away from her. I wonder how the lawyers will play it, with the spousal abuse in the background.

"I'm not a lawyer but I seem to remember there is a principle that if two people are at the scene of a killing and the evidence is not clear about which of the people present committed the crime, none of the suspects can be convicted," said Henry. "You know that 'beyond a reasonable doubt' stuff."

"I guess it's up to the lawyers if they get good ones," said Travers. "They may end up with lesser charges."

"I'll tell Staff Sergeant Glenn and DI Rowley," said Henry. But for us, we have confessions. Now we have reports to do."

Henry went to Staff Sergeant Glenn's office and told him what happened with Joan and Evelyn. Glenn congratulated Henry on a job well done - his bluff had paid off.

"I wish it would've had a clearer ending though," said Henry. "I can't win for losing. Who ends up with two credible confessions and doubts remaining!"

"You can let Alex McNeill go, poor kid," said Staff Sergeant Glenn. "I don't know how he is going to make sense of all this. Did we have other family members in the file?"

"I will talk to him and see," said Henry.

Chapter 24

Lisa was worried about Henry. She knew it had been a rough day, between the personal issues and the case. She asked Jeremy to go over and keep him company for a while. She didn't mention anything specific but she suggested Henry might enjoy seeing him again since it had been a while. When Jeremy saw Henry's car pull into his driveway he went over. He noticed Henry had a box with him and was curious.

"We've got the photos back Jeremy," said Henry. "And I know your mother told you about the letter from Scotland."

"Yes, that's great news. The photos are yours for good?"

"I have the paperwork, so they're mine," said Henry. "We can keep on working away. And we need to get going on the boat. I promised your sister, I'd take her boating before she goes to college!" laughed Henry.

Henry being the simple man that he was, had been hurt and there was a profound sadness. It could not be replaced easily by anything in his life now. Henry had to live in the present, he wasn't a dreamer.

"I got you a birthday present," said Henry. "I know it's next week, but I might as well give it to you now."

"You didn't have to you know," said Jeremy. "I'm not a kid anymore." But Henry could see he was curious and pleased.

Henry went to the garage and brought out a brand-new toolbox. "Open it."

Jeremy was thrilled, it wasn't a kid's present, it was a grown-up gift. His own toolbox, complete with all the basic tools for doing woodwork and repairs. He hesitated between shaking Henry's hand and hugging him. Finally, he went all out and hugged him. Henry smiled as Jeremy went to show Ellie and his mother.

For Henry affection was something he struggled with, it was unfamiliar. But he'd watched Lisa and the way she interacted with her children - the touching, the kissing, and the conversations. He admired that. Jeremy who claimed he was now too old for kisses from his mother, was affectionate with his baby sister. Henry had been born the fourth child in a family of seven, four boys and three girls. He had been labelled needy, and a crybaby. His father didn't take to that, feeling that boys shouldn't hold on to their mother's skirt. They had to be men from birth! His version of it anyway. With three more children after him, his mother had no time. They didn't linger in conversation or do bedtime stories. He was often teary-eyed and lost in the shuffle. The saving grace had been his older sister who took Henry under her wing. Fear of their father kept everyone in line. They ended up not being a close family and he only maintained rare contact with his sister. But his wife Paula had found ways to make that difficult.

Lisa came back to thank Henry for the present. She now had her own handyman. Jeremy was so happy about his present. "It's self-serving," said Henry. "We won't have to share the hammer and I can probably get more work out of him."

She asked him about the case and he told her about the confessions and how he felt sorry for Alex. To be left with another mess to sort out. She understood, and before leaving she reached out and kissed him. She moved closer to him and Henry returned her kiss, she let her hands run over his back. Henry moved away, and looked at her, "Is this your way of smoothing things over, your idea of affection for sympathy's sake? Do you feel sorry for me?"

"No, Henry, you don't understand," said Lisa. "I'm sorry if you think…"

"There might have been a time when I would have gone along with it, scraping by on what I could get," said Henry. "But now, I'm surprised to say this but I want more."

"It's not like that, Henry. But I see how you could think it is. Is there a way we can go back?"

"We can't change things," said Henry.

"But, like your computers, can we do a reset? Take a bit of time and see what happens next. The kids will always be your friends, it's just you and me that need to figure things out."

"Yes, me and you," said Henry. "Perhaps. It might be work."

"It might be fun," smiled Lisa as she left.

Chapter 25

Alex McNeill was released, and so was Joan for the moment. They would be called as witnesses. Gun charges were pending for Alex. He went to stay with his aunt and they re-opened the shop together. All the balls were in the lawyers' court for now, it would be a while before everything was settled. As Henry expected the abuse inflicted by Hugh McNeill on both his wife and son was brought as a mitigating factor. Evelyn had been arrested and faced murder charges but again the lawyers would plea for a lesser charge. She faced imprisonment. Alex and Joan were there to support her. They had other legal and financial matters to deal with.

DI Richard Rowley had written his final report before his retirement. Headquarters congratulated him on leading the investigation to a satisfactory conclusion.

Henry had been given his box of photos and had sent all the military pictures to the Scotland Military Museum in Kirknewton. It was in the general vicinity where the other photos were from. Encouraged by Lisa and Jeremy, Henry had written to a local newspaper in Uphall Station to ask for help in finding any relatives of the people he had identified in the photos. They ran an article about this Canadian man with local photos. It took a while and many exchanged letters, but Henry managed to link with the granddaughter of one of the boys in the family prints. They had been taken in front of the miner's cottage where the family had lived. He had sent her a few photos to start and she confirmed the identification of everyone and even provided more background to them. Eventually, Henry sent her everything.

Patrick Jones and his wife Judy had a baby girl. Henry took Lisa for a visit; she had met Judy at the barbecue. He took Lisa's suggestion for a baby present and brought the baby an assortment of little shoes and slippers. It was an unusual gift but it was needed and the baby would grow into them. Judy agreed and loved them, especially the little sneakers.

Following the visit, rumours were circulating in the station that Henry and Lisa were an item. It was not the case but Henry didn't fight the whispers very hard. It gave him a bit of prestige around the coffee pot and stopped any further invitations to join *a Parents Without Partners* meeting. To everyone's surprise, Randy Travers was still seeing the beautician from Cornwall. His hair had grown back, and there had been no further experimentation with the eyebrows. Henry was happy for him, although he still secretly hoped Travers would find love with a lady in the food industry, preferably a bakery. For now, Travers would go back to his detachment in Long Sault.

Henry received his divorce papers, to his great relief. Paula had gone over the abortion issue with her lawyer and to avoid further embarrassment and discussions, she did not confront Lisa or threaten her job. Both lawyers negotiated a further financial offer. They went over the value of both houses, divided that in half and considered the $40,000 plus interest the Canada Savings Bond had brought in for Paula. Henry had to throw a few more dollars at her, but it was a sum he could manage. She would not touch his pension. He had not seen Paula and did not wish to. The hurt was still there. He would come to forgive her but he would not forget. Looking at Lisa and her children, he came to understand why Paula didn't want children. She would have been incapable of nurturing them. The child would have been fed and clean but he doubted Paula had the necessary selflessness to be a good mother. He also saw the difficulty in their marriage. They had never talked, never resolved any issues, they pretended instead.

One quiet evening, Henry picked up the phone and called his sister Michelle. She lived in Montreal, and luckily for him had kept the same number over the years. She was so pleased to hear from him and Henry realized just how much he had missed her. They talked for over an hour, catching up on both their lives. Michelle was also divorced, her two children out of the house at college and working. She told him she had been doing genealogy and had photos of their ancestors to show him. She congratulated him on his divorce and planned to come up to Winchester for a visit in the coming weeks. That would give Henry enough time to sort out the house and the spare bedroom. He now had his very own next of kin!

Transfers and promotions notices had circulated in the office and Jones had shown some interest. Henry would be sad to see him go, but it was a natural progression and Jones was good at his job. Henry did not even read them; he was simply fine where he was. He was even up for putting in a few more years with Travers, the man was never boring at least.

The boat building was not going well, and with fall just around the corner, Henry would not see water this year. He found he didn't care for it very much now. If Ellie wanted to float around, they could always rent a pedal boat at Dow's Lake in Ottawa. That would be a fun day out. Instead, and now that Jeremy had his monogrammed toolbox of his own, they could start updating Lisa's house. Since Henry owned it, it would keep his investment in good standing. Jeremy suggested they could fix up the basement and put in a bedroom for him with a sitting area for video games and movies when his friends came over. Lisa suggested the kitchen could use a makeover and Ellie wanted more shelves for her toys. Henry and Jeremy made a list, shifting priorities up and down, he could always teach the boy and let him work on small projects.

Nothing was happening at work, and it was a blessing. The most exciting thing that happened since the murder investigation was the new vending machines. Installed from a new supplier who claimed to respect freshness and expiry dates. Prices had also gone up.

Wes, the ambulance driver, asked Lisa out a few more times. He had accumulated a slew of coupon books and was ready to treat her to a wild night out. She declined on all accounts.

Conclusion

McHaffie Flea Market just north of Morrisburg was a Sunday event that had been growing in popularity. The number of vendors increased steadily and Henry dropped in every so often to look for additions to his photo collection. He knew Jeremy was interested in coming along, so he also asked Lisa and Ellie. It was a short drive from Winchester. Henry believed that flea market attendance was like golf, you either loved it or you hated it. For some it was all junk, for others, it was undiscovered treasures. Shoppers had strategies, like waiting for a few minutes before closing time to make an offer a vendor found hard to refuse. Henry wasn't much of a bargainer. If he wanted something and he felt the price was right for him, he bought it. He'd seen people haggle over a dollar and walk away if a vendor didn't budge. That wasn't his idea of fun.

Henry and Lisa walked with Ellie holding hands in between them. Jeremy, as it turned out, was quite taken by booth number 5, a kitchenware vendor. Lisa knew he had no interest in pots and pans but the vendor's daughter was another matter. When he came back to join them, Henry teased him about it.

"She's both cute and fun," said Jeremy. "That's what you told me was the best choice Henry, remember?"

"Henry Stafford are you giving my son advice on women and dating?" asked Lisa. She couldn't help but laugh.

"Those who can, do; those who can't, teach," said Henry.

Ellie tugged at his hand. She was fascinated with everything at the market and showed an interest in some stamps, those with cats and butterflies on them. Henry bought her a few packages and an album for collecting. Lisa had a keen eye for photos and directed Henry to a few interesting pieces. She loved the food vendors and got some baked goods. It was a pleasant day.

In the fall, just before the closing of the flea market, Henry asked them again. Lisa came along, but Ellie was with her father and Jeremy was at Sutton's, bowling with his friends. They did the usual rounds, Henry checked for new stamps for Ellie and Lisa picked up pies that she would freeze for later.

They stopped for a coffee and Henry looked at her attentively. She was chatting away about funny vendors and browsers. He thought she was pretty and that he should kiss her. This was a public place, so in a way, kissing was safe, if discreet. He couldn't be too involved or too long, and if it didn't work out, they could just move along. Kissing in public didn't create an obligation then and there so it couldn't go further. Would she mind? After all, she had kissed him already, so obviously she didn't mind. How badly did he want it? He remembered he didn't like to take risks. Henry's psyche was still debating "kissing" versus "no kissing," each side holding strong in the arm-wrestling contest. The United

Nations made quicker decisions. Lisa got up to go back and browse the stalls. Lucky for Henry, she took his hand as they walked.

Once again, faith has saved him from making, yet another life-changing decision, too easy he thought. But he remembered what he had said to Jeremy, "…you need to take a more active part in your life." In a bold move, which took Henry to the edge of his insecurities, he stopped, turned around and looked at Lisa.

"What?" she asked.

Henry touched her thick brown hair and moved closer, right there in aisle C in front of the stall selling hubcaps, he kissed her. He felt her surprise but she didn't seem to mind at all. He smiled. The Happiness Train had pulled up once more, and this time he didn't even have a ticket. He walked up and took the conductor's seat. "All aboard," he heard down the track.

The second book in this series is in the works!

For release date and other information please go to my website www.ginetteguymayer.com.

Manufactured by Amazon.ca
Bolton, ON